OTHER WORKS by JESSICA DALE

The Unintended Consequences Trilogy
PAYBACK
BACKLASH
BACKFIRE

~~

The Binding Love Duet
Binding Vows
Binding Choice

~~

Bartered Innocence, A Romantic Thriller

OTHER SERIES by KASSANDRA LAMB

The Kate Huntington Mysteries
Psychotherapist Kate Huntington helps others cope with trauma, but she has led a charmed life...until a killer rips it apart. (10 novels) ~ Plus 4 **Kate on Vacation** novellas.

~~

The Marcia Banks and Buddy Cozy Mysteries
Marcia Banks trains service dogs for veterans, and solves crimes on the side, with the help of her Black Lab, Buddy. (13 novels/novellas)

~~

The C.o.P. on the Scene Mysteries
Eight days into her new job as Chief of Police in a small Florida city, Judith Anderson finds herself one step behind a serial killer. (spinoff from the Kate Huntington series; 3 stories–more to come)

BACKLASH

An Unintended Consequences
Romantic Suspense
Kassandra Lamb, writing as JESSICA
DALE

a misterio press publication

Published by Dark Ardor Publications, a subsidiary of *misterio press LLC*

Cover design by Melinda VanLone, Book Cover Corner

Backlash is a work of fiction. All names, characters, events, and most places are products of the author's imagination. Any resemblance to actual people, living or dead, or the events in their lives is entirely coincidental. Some real places are used fictitiously. Paxtonburg, Virginia and Paxton County are fictitious locations

The publisher has no control over and does not assume any responsibility for third-party websites and their content.

CHAPTER ONE

Carrie

For the half-second before the dog reacted, I assumed the person ringing the doorbell was James, arriving for dinner.

Then Ginger went ballistic.

Heart pounding, I quickly lowered the flame under the sauce and power-walked into the living room, trying to convince myself that it wasn't Greg at the door.

I really had to get a handle on my fear. This was no way to live.

The tinkle of wind chimes in a slight breeze somehow reassured me. I'd gotten used to the sound, even though I owned no wind chimes and, despite its age, my house was not particularly drafty.

The doorbell rang again and Ginger raced ahead of me to sniff at the crack between the front door and its jamb. Another burst of ear-splitting barks bounced off the walls of the near-empty room.

Definitely not James. He only rang the bell once before using his own key, so as not to scare me when he came in.

My chest so tight I could hardly breathe, I scrunched down a little to look through the door's peephole, originally installed for a shorter woman. My hand flew to my mouth to stifle a scream. Bile rose in the back of my throat.

Wait! Greg's features, yes, and brown hair like his, lighter than my dark auburn, but...

The face was younger, with dark stubble on boyish cheeks and wide eyes staring back at me—the same sky blue as my own.

I fumbled with the locks and threw the door open. "Philly!"

He grinned shyly and ducked his head a little. "Hi, Mom."

James

My mind was elsewhere, not quite worrying but definitely thinking about the auditions I had lined up over the next week. It was always nerve-racking to be between plays. I rounded the front corner of the old farmhouse and stopped cold, unable at first to process the scene before me.

Carrie didn't know any local men well enough to be hugging them, except me of course. Therefore, this man was from her past, which did not bode well despite the hug.

My stomach hollowed out and my heart beat faster.

Was this Greg? Was she the type of woman who ran back into her ex's arms the minute he was kind to her?

I felt nauseous.

Ginger shoved between Carrie's leg and the doorjamb and trotted over to me. I absently patted the golden retriever's head as I watched Carrie take the man by the shoulders and nudge him a bit away from her.

No, more a boy really. My insides unknotted some, but my heart hammered harder. Not Greg, but still not good.

"Look at you," Carrie said with a big smile.

I stepped up onto the end of the porch that stretched across the front of her house, my footsteps dull thuds on the wooden floorboards.

The kid startled and immediately pivoted to put himself between me and Carrie, a reflexive move that should *not* be instinctive in a teenage boy.

He was almost as tall as me, already five-ten at least, but slender. I doubted he weighed more than a hundred pounds. His blue eyes, so like Carrie's, were wide in a boy-man face.

Carrie nudged him aside and waved for me to approach. "James, this is my son. Phillip, this is my neighbor and friend, James Fitzgerald."

The *son*, at this point, didn't surprise me, but the *friend* did a little. We were a hell of a lot more than friends.

But hey, it's her kid. I'll follow her lead. I stuck out my hand. "Pleased to meet you, Phillip."

He mumbled something that I didn't catch, as I used the handshake to turn him toward the open front door. I began to herd them inside. "Best not to be standing around out here," I said without thinking.

Carrie's delighted expression deflated like a popped balloon, and I felt like a heel. I could've let her enjoy her reunion with her son a few minutes longer before reminding her of the threat that reunion represented.

I glanced around for Ginger. She was busily searching the wide expanse of front lawn—a field really, that I mowed with my John Deere—looking for just the right spot.

I left her to her business. She wouldn't go far. An invisible fence encircled the field, the house and the smaller yard and garden in the back.

Once the humans were all inside, with the door closed and locked behind us, Carrie laid a palm against Phillip's cheek. "I can't believe it. You're shaving."

His cheeks turned pink under the smattering of dark hairs. "Actually I left home in February." He rubbed his stubbled chin. "This started a few weeks ago..." He trailed off, his expression part pleased, part sheepish.

The pleased made sense. Every boy looks forward to his first whiskers as a sign of manhood. But why sheepish?

I got it with a jolt. My throat tightened. *And every boy should have a man in his life to teach him to shave.*

Even my old man had stepped up to fulfill that role. It was one of the few times he'd acted like he cared.

"Hey," I said, "you two catch up for a few minutes. I forgot something."

I went back out the front door. Ginger trotted up onto the porch and licked my hand. I let her into the house, then locked the door.

I scanned the stretches of grass on either side of the gravel lane leading down to Carrie's and my houses. They were beginning to green up after a long winter. Then I moved my gaze to the strip of woods up by the main road. No signs of movement and no sounds that didn't belong.

Just a bird chirping in the tree beside my garage. A good sign.

A cool breeze brought the scent of damp earth to my nostrils. I headed across our lawns to my own front porch.

A few minutes later, carrying a small paper bag, I let myself in Carrie's door with my key. Her house was sporadically furnished with things she'd found or bought cheap at yard sales. The only furniture in the living room was a second-hand leather sofa.

Carrie and Phillip were sitting in the middle of it. She held his hand and their heads were bent together. The boy was chattering away—something about school—gesturing with his other hand. His voice, cracking occasionally, bounced off the walls of the cavernous room.

She looked so damned happy that I couldn't help smiling, even though the implications of his presence were terrifying.

I walked past them and followed my nose to the "modern" kitchen that had been tacked onto the back of the house in the early 1970s. I saved the spaghetti sauce from burning with a quick stir, turned down the heat under the pan of boiling water and dumped a whole box of pasta into it. Half was usually enough for Carrie and me, but her son was still a growing boy.

I was trying to remember his age. Fourteen or fifteen?

I foraged in the fridge. I'd made a salad and was cutting the garlic bread retrieved from the oven when mother and son came into the kitchen, arms around each other's waists.

I'd placed wineglasses at two places on the rickety wooden table in the breakfast nook and a glass of milk at the other. The paper bag sat on that plate. I made eye contact with Phillip and gestured toward that place.

"What's this?" the boy said, picking up the bag.

"Some stuff your mom can show you how to use later." I'd decided his mother would be a more acceptable tutor than a man he'd just met. I kept my eyes diverted as I dished up pasta and sauce on the three plates.

When I glanced up, Phillip was peering into the bag at the disposable razor and can of shaving cream inside. "Thanks, man." He gave me a shy smile.

"You're welcome. Let's eat."

Good that I'd scored points right out of the gate with the kid. Because once we'd eaten, I'd have to grill him on how he'd found his mother and what kind of trail he'd left for his father to follow.

——◦——

Carrie

I could hardly eat. Excitement and terror had my stomach twisted into knots.

I also couldn't take my eyes off my son. He'd grown at least an inch in the nine months since I'd left him with his father and run for my life.

"So…" I struggled to push the words past my lips. "So how is your dad?" I didn't really care how he was—only *where* he was—but it was the polite thing to say.

Phillip grimaced. "He's got a new girlfriend. Toni with an *i*," he sneered.

He stopped to gobble down a fork full of spaghetti. I wondered how long it had been since he'd had a good meal. My chest ached.

"When he moved her in, I knew I had to get out of there. Sorry, Mom, but I couldn't take it anymore." His eyes pleaded for understanding. "I'd been saving my money to buy a new Play Station. I bought a bus ticket instead."

My heart was in my throat, imagining my son by himself on a dirty bus. Anything could have happened to him? Some sleaze could have…

"How did you find your mother?" James asked.

I suspected he'd been waiting for an opening. I shot him a grateful look. I couldn't bring myself to question Phillip. I was so damn glad to see him.

"I didn't start looking for her until after I'd left home." His voice was slightly defensive as he answered James. He turned his gaze toward me. "I went to Grandmom's town first, but I didn't go to see her. I just asked around to find out if you'd been there."

I guess I should have felt bad about not letting my mother know I was still alive and well, but I hadn't trusted her not to tell Greg whatever I told her. She'd always liked Greg and didn't seem to totally believe me when I'd told her about the beatings.

And did I really owe her anything when it was her bitterness that had driven me into Greg's arms in the first place?

"I remembered you telling me about that summer in rural Virginia," Phillip was saying, "when you were twelve, and how much you loved it."

James looked at me, eyes wide, lips in a grim line. I shook my head, silently answering his question. No, I'd never told Greg about that summer vacation.

"So I got another bus to Richmond," my son said, "and started making circles around there, stopping in each small town and asking if anyone had seen you."

"How did you get around?" I demanded.

"Mostly I walked." He ducked his head, avoiding eye contact. "And hitchhiked a couple of times."

My stomach hollowed out. "Nobody messed with you, did they?"

He shook his head. "I had a picture of you that I showed people." He extracted a tattered photo from his shirt pocket and handed it to me.

My younger self stared up at me, her arm around ten-year-old Phillip's shoulders.

"Dad burned all the photo albums, but you'd given me a copy of that one."

James was still looking at me, alarm on his face.

Phillip finally noticed. "What? Did I do something wrong?"

I grabbed my son's hand and gave it a squeeze. "No, no. Everything's fine."

But of course, it wasn't. He'd laid a trail a blind man could follow.

CHAPTER TWO

James

After the three of us had cleaned up the kitchen, Carrie gave me a big hug. "Thanks for salvaging dinner," she said in a too-loud voice. "I'll call you in the morning."

I took that to mean she wasn't ready to tell Phillip about us, although the kid seemed bright enough to have figured something out by now.

The hug left my jeans uncomfortably tight, but I smiled graciously and said goodnight to both of them. Being an actor has its advantages in private life sometimes.

I walked carefully across the dark stretch of lawn between our houses, my eyes shifting back and forth between the uneven ground in front of me and the strip of woods at the edge of the front field. A slight breeze stirred in the treetops and the moonlight created shadows that could hide an army of pissed-off husbands.

What was I thinking getting involved with a married woman? In Carrie's mind the marriage was over, but I doubted Greg Peterson felt that way.

Granted he'd moved on to another woman, but even if he didn't care about Carrie anymore, she'd wounded his pride. In my experience, abusive men didn't let that go.

The old man's pride had certainly been a wall between us. Even as a college student, I wasn't allowed to voice my own opinions if they differed the slightest from his. "In *my* house," the man I'd thought was my father had bellowed, "you will respect the values you were raised by." Those "values" included a belief that he was superior to anyone who wasn't male, white, straight and at least upper middle-class. Finally my answer to his disdain for most of the human race was to leave his house completely, and not return until after he and my mother were dead.

It wasn't until many years later I'd discovered he wasn't my biological father.

I entered that house I had once forsaken and now owned. A warm flow of air—which I was pretty sure had nothing to do with my heating system—enveloped me as I walked into the kitchen. My lips curled into a slight smile.

"Hi, Mom," I said out loud. The warmth intensified.

I pulled out my phone, sat down at the table and punched a speed dial number.

"Hey James, how are you?" Mary's voice sounded more chipper than it had in a long time.

As we exchanged small talk for a moment, I visualized her slender face, bracketed by blonde hair, her blue eyes soft and warm with friendship. Her too thin body was probably already wrapped in a robe, even though it wasn't quite eight o'clock yet. Mary wasn't much of a night person.

Why couldn't I have fallen for this simple soul, instead of the complicated woman next door? I immediately felt guilty for the thought.

"Hey Mare, I need your help with something."

She was a paralegal for a law firm in DC, and she had the resources to do background checks. Plus she was a whiz in general regarding all things internet-related. I told her about Carrie's son finding her, and that he'd probably led his father right to us.

"What are you going to do?" The panic in Mary's voice resonated off my own fear, amplifying it.

I paused, took a deep breath. "I don't know yet. She and I didn't get a chance to discuss it."

"Okay," Mary said. "I'll see what I can find out about this Gregory Peterson. Where will you be tomorrow?"

That was a very good question. I was supposed to drive to DC in the afternoon and spend the night at my apartment there, so I could be bright-eyed and brilliant for an audition on Thursday morning. But I was more than a little hesitant about leaving Carrie right now.

"I'm not sure. Best to call my cell."

"Got it. And, James, try not to worry too much. I'm sure everything will work out okay."

I wasn't at all sure of that, but I thanked Mary and signed off.

My bed was cold. My body ached for Carrie. I got up and read for a bit, drank another glass of wine. Finally I was sleepy enough to go back to bed.

But it still took awhile for me to drift off.

Wake up! A whisper. The gentle tinkling of wind chimes.

The sounds were so soft, I wasn't sure if I'd heard them, or just dreamt them.

I opened one eye. The light filtering through my bedroom curtains was dim. It couldn't be much past sunrise.

I was debating whether to try for more sleep when a rustling sound near my dresser jolted me fully awake. I turned my head in time to see the bedroom door closing.

Out of bed in an instant, I yanked the door open, but there was no one in the hallway.

Nothing but one of my ghosts. I pulled my head back inside the room.

The sounds of someone running down the stairs, then a door closing. The ghosts that shared my house didn't bother with doors.

I pulled the bedroom door open wider, about to give chase, when something caught my eye on the dresser. A piece of paper, folded in half, propped against a bottle of cologne.

I grabbed it and scanned the words inside.

Dear James, We haven't said the word out loud yet, but know that I love you with all my heart, which is why I can't put you at risk. Phillip and I are going elsewhere, until I can...

The words blurred. A vise closed around my chest.

Crumpling the note, I bolted down the stairs and out into the morning chill in nothing but my pajama bottoms. The goose bumps on my arms and chest barely registered.

Phillip was climbing into the passenger side of Carrie's car. She was in the driver's seat.

Some maniac screamed inside my head. *Noooo!*

I sprinted across my lawn. "Wait!" I yelled.

She ignored me and started the car.

No, dear God, no! I had to stop her. The thought that she would drive away and I would never see her again terrified me.

I made it to the gravel road that led to both our houses as she was pulling out of her driveway. Standing in the middle of the road, ignoring the rocks biting into my bare feet and the cool breeze that made me shiver, I spread my arms wide.

She crept toward me. Phillip stuck his head out his window. "She says to get out of the way," he called out.

I shook my head. Pressure built in my chest, one part anger, one part panic. "You're gonna have to run me over," I yelled at her wide-eyed face behind the windshield.

She waited until she was close, then swerved off onto the grass and gunned it.

I threw myself across her hood, almost sliding off the other side. Grabbing her windshield wiper, I hung on. The car screeched to a halt, plastering me against the windshield and then almost throwing me off the hood.

Relief made my muscles weak for a moment. She'd stopped the car.

The driver's door flew open and she jumped out. "James, what are you doing? You could've been killed."

I lifted my head and looked up into her eyes. "You. Are. Not. Leaving. Me."

I swung my legs around and landed in front of her. Grabbing her shoulders, I shook her. I couldn't remember when I'd been this angry.

The crunch of Phillip's sneakers on the gravel as he rounded the car. "Let her go!"

The terror in her eyes registered.

What the hell am I doing? I yanked my hands away from her shoulders as if they were on fire.

Her eyes cleared. She shifted her weight.

She's getting back in the car! I reached past her and snatched the keys from the ignition.

Ginger whined from one side of the backseat. The vise around my chest tightened at the sight of suitcases piled high on the other side.

Phillip grabbed my arm, tried to pull me away from the car and his mother.

"Philly, it's okay," Carrie said.

The kid's grip loosened.

I forced myself to take a deep breath—the vise made it difficult—then gently shook him off. "We need to talk," I said carefully. "All of us. Phillip, bring the dog."

Her keys still firmly clutched in my hand, I turned on my heel and marched across the driveway, trying not to react to the gravel poking the soles of my bare feet. Shivering, I strode toward my porch.

Once inside the front door, my chest started heaving. I tried for another deep breath, but the vise around my rib cage wouldn't allow it. I shivered more violently.

Carrie found me sitting on the ladderback chair in my foyer, head in my hands, shoulders shaking from the effort of holding in sobs.

She knelt in front of my chair and wrapped her arms around me. "I'm sorry, James. I'm so sorry. It wasn't for forever, just until I could get things straightened out."

The warmth of her arms barely penetrated my chilled torso, as if a wall had gone up between us.

I raised my head. "And if he'd found you," I pushed past the tightness in my throat, "and *killed* you, I never would've known."

She sat back on her heels, her face pale, eyes wide. "I didn't think of that," she whispered.

Phillip appeared in the open doorway, his mouth hanging open, the dog's leash in his hand. I ignored him. Whether Carrie liked it or not, he was about to find out what his mother meant to me.

"I have loved three women in my life. I lost the first two. My mother and my best friend *died!*" I choked a little on the word. "And now you were going to..." My throat closed completely and my vision blurred.

Soft palms touched my cheeks. "Oh, James. I do love you."

I blinked in time to see her eyes close as she kissed me on the lips. It was the lightest of kisses but it stopped my shivering. My groin stirred.

Phillip cleared his throat. "Uh, Mom, ya want me to unload the car?"

She turned her head and smiled up at her son. "Yes, that would be very helpful. James and I need to talk."

The boy nodded and grabbed the doorknob.

But talking was not what my body had in mind. As soon as the door had closed, I wrapped my arms around her and pulled her onto my lap.

Carrie

I wasn't as contrite as I pretended to be. Oh, I was truly sorry that I'd hurt James. I hadn't realized how deeply my leaving would affect him—although I should have. His mother had betrayed him, chosen his stepfather over him, and Annaleise and her husband had been brutally murdered, in James's own house. How could he *not* have abandonment issues?

But mostly I regretted not leaving the note in his kitchen as I'd originally intended. I hadn't been able to resist taking one more look at his lean body, his face soft with sleep, his dark hair tousled.

If I'd been stronger, Phillip and I would be long gone.

If I were stronger, perhaps I would have stopped James before he started making love to me. His lips on mine, he tugged my shirt loose from my waistband and hastily unbuttoned it. His hands pushed my bra up and cupped my breasts.

His palms were warm and slightly rough against the nipples, sending currents sizzling through my body. Throbbing heat pooled in my core.

My God, this man could make me feel things I'd never felt before.

"James," I gasped. "Now is not the time."

"You want me to stop?" he said in a low, gravelly voice.

My brain said yes, but a low moan came out of my mouth. My hands gripping his bare, muscular shoulders, I shook my head slightly.

A soft chuckle and his mouth found mine again.

James and I, hand in hand, crossed our adjacent lawns.

Phillip was pulling his duffle bag out of the car. He slammed the trunk closed. The sound reverberated off the trees.

"I put everything in the living room," he said as we approached, his voice carefully even. He looked at our clasped hands and his eyes narrowed. "Want me to put the stuff away?"

James loosened his grip, started to pull his hand free of mine. I held onto it.

"No, leave everything there for now," I said. "Would you mind hanging out in the study while James and I talk?" It's where he had slept the night before, on the old discarded sofa bed I'd retrieved from the side of the road two months ago.

Phillip gave me a defiant look, as if to say, *I thought you'd already "talked."*

My cheeks heated. I opened my mouth, although I had no idea what I would say to get us past the awkward moment.

"He has a right to be in on this." James tugged me partway around to face him. "Just as I have a right to be in on this." His voice was firm, but his eyes were pleading, begging me not to shut him out.

Guilt and joy did battle in my chest. My eyes stung. I nodded silently, not trusting my voice right then.

Once we were settled in the kitchen with cups of coffee in front of us, James cleared his throat. "First, Phillip, I'd like to apologize for losing my temper like that. I know you have no reason to trust this yet, but I am not a violent man."

James turned his head toward me. "I only use physical force when absolutely necessary to protect myself or those I love."

A faint tinkling sound half registered in the back of my mind.

I gave James a slight nod, acknowledging the day we had vowed never to speak of again, when we had both used violence to protect each other from a killer.

James

My throat closed again at the thought of how close I'd come to losing this woman. I wanted to rail at her. How could she leave me?

But her son's presence stopped me, thank God—kept me from making a fool of myself. Or starting a fight and scaring her again.

We needed to focus on the common enemy. My lover's husband.

I turned my gaze to Phillip. Could he be trusted, when it came down to it, to fight off his own father?

"So do we stay or run?" the boy asked.

"I vote for stay," I said without giving it much thought.

Carrie's eyes went wide, anxiety flickering in them.

I quickly added, "It's mainly up to your mother, though." I wrapped both my hands around hers. "I'll go with you if you want to leave. But whatever we do, we do it together."

"Where could we go?" Her eyes still wide, she fixated on my face.

A surge of fear for her threatened to loosen my bowels. I'd somehow believed this day wouldn't come. That we were safe, hidden away in the Virginia woods. Now that denial had been ripped away, and I was feeling some of what she had felt for most of her adult life. Waiting for the monster to appear, to inflict pain, perhaps to kill this time.

"To Grandmom's?" Phillip's voice, hesitant, broke the spell.

Carrie shook her head. "No, she's..." Her voice trailed off. She pulled a hand loose from mine to push her thick auburn hair back from her face. "Sorry, Phillip, she's your grandmother and I know you love her, but she's taken your father's side too many times. She can't be trusted."

Phillip nodded, his expression more solemn than any kid's should ever be. Then his face brightened slightly. "Maybe we shouldn't pick a logical place to go. If we do, then Dad can probably figure out the logic as well. He's not stupid."

I looked at the boy with new respect. He was no dummy either. "So maybe," I said, "we go to Richmond airport and pick a flight at random."

Carrie shook her head again. "James, I can't ask you to give up everything like that, your home, your career."

I opened my mouth to protest, to voice the commitment to go anywhere with her and to keep her safe, when another thought froze the words in my throat. We couldn't leave a trail. How could I pay for that flight to wherever, and for a new life there, if I couldn't access my bank accounts or use my credit cards?

Carrie had some money stashed, an inheritance from an aunt that she'd been able to live off of only because she got cheap rent in exchange for renovating the old house. It wouldn't be enough to support all of us for very long.

How could I claim this woman and her son if I couldn't take care of them?

I'll dig ditches, if need be.

Out loud, I said, "One thing I know…" I heard the catch in my voice, stopped to gain control of it. I was about to repeat my "we're in this together" mantra.

But Carrie interrupted. "I'd never intended to hide forever. I was waiting until Phillip was older, and for Greg to get over his anger some." She turned toward her son. "The plan was to file for custody after your next birthday."

I squeezed her hand. "It would be hard to file for custody without a permanent mailing address."

Carrie gave me a wan smile. "I think I'm tired of running. How about you, Phillip?"

The boy nodded. "I vote to stay."

"Okay. Then please put away the things from the car."

"No problem."

Carrie's eyes followed her son as he jumped up and left the room. When he was well out of earshot, she said, "How long do you think we have?"

I swallowed hard. "One to three days."

CHAPTER THREE

James

The vise-around-my-chest feeling returned at the thought of anything happening to Carrie, or to her son. "I think we need to go see Uncle Sammy today. Get things rolling legally, and get a restraining order in place."

Carrie nodded silently and got up to make breakfast.

After we'd eaten, I lobbied for Phillip to stay at the house. I was relatively sure Greg wouldn't track down our location quite yet, and the conversation with Sam would be a lot easier without him there.

"You've got to be exhausted," I said to the boy.

I hadn't counted on the energy of youth. Phillip insisted he felt fine.

We drove into town in my Mustang. Phillip's eyes had lit up when he saw it. "Can I sit up front?" he'd asked, while stroking the shiny black fender.

I glanced at Carrie. "Sure."

I said no to putting the top down though. Mother Nature seemed to have forgotten that we were past the spring equinox. A cool breeze blew dry leaves across the front field as I climbed into the driver's seat.

I'd called ahead. Sam was waiting for us, his portly frame filling the doorway of his office, an unlit stogie in the corner of his mouth. While his admin watched with an indulgent expression, he shook my hand and hugged Carrie.

The overhead lights reflected off the shiny scalp showing through Sam's thinning gray hair as he turned to Phillip. He grabbed the boy's hand and pumped it. "Aren't you a fine young man!"

He led us into his office and gestured toward three leather, barrel chairs, arranged in a semi-circle in front of his mahogany desk. We all sat. Sam perched reading glasses on his nose and picked up an expensive-looking pen.

"So we need a protective order." He looked at Carrie over his glasses.

She nodded.

"How long you been separated?" Sam asked.

"I left a little over nine months ago. I moved around for a few weeks, covering my trail, and then rented my house here last August."

Sam smiled at her around the stogie. "Good, so you've been a Virginia resident for over six months. We just gotta wait 'til a year is up from the date you left, to file for divorce. But we can get temporary custody now. You need supervised visitation?"

I snorted. "I don't think that's necessary. Phillip has shown us his ability to get away from his father if need be."

The boy gave me a small smile.

"Right," Sam said. "No need to aggravate the situation anymore than we hafta."

He dropped his pen and took off his glasses. "Y'all oughta come into town and stay with Maisie and me."

I'd anticipated that reaction. "Thanks for the invite, Uncle Sammy." I used the honorary title intentionally—Sam was my late stepfather's law partner. "But Carrie's house is a fortress. We'll be okay."

"Harumpf." Sam picked up his pen and glasses again. He asked Carrie and Phillip several questions, taking notes on a lined, yellow pad. "Okay," he finally said, "I'll have this drawn up by later this afternoon. I'll give y'all a call."

I knew that was way faster than most things happened in a law office. I stood and grinned at Sam. "Thanks."

He pushed his bulk out of his seat and shook my hand.

Carrie

We were no sooner out of the lawyer's office than I had an anxiety attack.

Filing for custody meant that Greg would be served with papers. What if he didn't care that I was gone? Or maybe even that Phillip had taken off? He had the type of twisted male ego that might decide his son wasn't worth his trouble if the boy dared to run away from him.

Getting served would only stir him up, enrage him that we dared to defy him.

And Sam's office address would be on the papers. Greg would assume we lived nearby.

I managed to keep it together until we got home. Then I asked Phillip to hang out in the study for a bit while James and I talked about something personal. He was more than happy to immerse himself in video games on my computer.

The sounds of battle in some virtual alien world, bouncing off the study ceiling, filtered through the kitchen wall. The half vaulted ceilings in both rooms, complete with rustic rafters, had probably been all the rage when some diligent

Harry Homeowner had built the back extension. Now they were outdated and created an annoying echo chamber.

We settled at the kitchen table, James with coffee, me with chamomile tea. I stared up at the kitchen rafters—noting that they needed to be revarnished—as I gathered my courage. James and Sam had gone to a lot of trouble.

"I'm not sure filing papers is a good idea," I said.

James cocked his head. "Why not?" His tone was slightly incredulous.

"Well, it's like waving a red flag at Greg. And it'll make it that much easier for him to find–."

The wind chimes interrupted, clamoring loudly.

I jerked, my knee, hitting the table's leg. Coffee and tea slopped onto its surface.

James's eyes went wide. "You can hear it?"

I nodded and opened my mouth to ask what it was.

Ginger erupted in the living room.

James

We both jumped up and raced through the house.

Carrie got to Ginger first. The dog had her head stuck between the curtains covering the big bay window. Sharp, staccato barks punctuated periods of rumbling deep in her throat.

One hand on Ginger's head, the other holding aside the curtain, Carrie stared out the window.

I stepped up to the other side of the window, nudged aside the curtain and scanned the two yards and the front field. Nothing seemed out of place.

I raised my gaze to the strip of woods along the roadside, a quarter mile from our houses.

Carrie was petting Ginger, telling her she was a good girl, trying to get her to calm down. The dog was having none of it.

There were shadows under the trees. A few of those shadows moved slightly, but that could just be a breeze rustling the limbs.

Finally Ginger quieted. I was about to suggest that a squirrel had set her off when a light flashed from under the trees, so fleeting I thought I might be imagining it.

"What's going on?" Phillip's voice from behind us.

I'd heard the boy coming, but Carrie jumped. She didn't take her eyes off the woods though.

"You see it too?" I said in a low voice.

She nodded.

The light flashed again.

We both stepped back from the window, Carrie almost colliding with her son.

"Where's your pistol?" I asked. Technically it was my pistol, purchased from the gun store in town. Carrie couldn't risk a background check since her driver's license was a fake.

Her previous pistol, which she'd bought illegally, was now in the hands of the county sheriff. I'd claimed it had belonged to my stepfather, that I'd found it when I'd inherited the house, but Sheriff Wallace had confiscated it anyway.

"In my bedroom." Carrie's voice shook a little. She turned and headed up the stairs.

I stared at Phillip. "If this comes to a pitched battle, where are you gonna be standing?"

The topic had come up, sort of, in Sam's office. He'd asked the boy if he was sure he could testify in court against his father regarding the beatings his mother had endured.

Phillip met my gaze, his eyes hard, his mouth pressed into a tight line. "You don't know how many times I've wanted to kill him," he clenched his fists, "when he was whaling on her. I tried to stop him once..." His eyes pooled with tears. "He picked me up by the shoulders and put me aside, like I was a toothpick or something."

His words seethed with anger, but this was his father out there. My fear was that he'd have a last minute change of heart.

"Whatever you do," I said, "don't get between him and whoever's holding the pistol. If you got hurt, it would destroy your mother."

His face paled and his shoulders slumped. "This is real, isn't it? We may have to kill him."

My throat tightened at the quaver in his voice, but I was pleased to hear the *we*. "Yeah, it may come to that."

Carrie walked up behind him, the pistol in her hand, down at her side. Multiple emotions flashed across her face, so jumbled it was hard to pinpoint them, but guilt was the predominant one in her eyes. She opened her mouth, then closed it again.

"What do we do now?" Phillip asked.

"We wait," I said. "Once the restraining order is in place, we can call the sheriff and get him to check the woods for trespassers." I resisted the urge to ask Carrie if she still thought the restraining order was a bad idea.

She sent Phillip back to his video games in the study.

Despite the grim reality that the flashing light in the woods represented, I was grateful for the interruption to our conversation. I wasn't ready to tell Carrie about the wind chimes.

Because when I did, I might lose her.

Carrie

Sitting with James on the living room sofa, I tried not to stare at the front door, expecting it to fly open at any moment. Already the waiting was grating on my nerves.

Ginger was at our feet, the pistol beside me on a pillow.

James was now almost as good a shot as I was. We'd practiced frequently in the field behind our houses. I'd shown him how to stand and to hold the gun with both hands, just as my gun-enthusiast father had taught my brother and me when we were barely into our teens.

James could now take out a tin can eight times out of ten at twenty feet, pulling the gun up from his side and taking no more than a second to aim.

But I felt better with the gun beside me. And I knew Ginger would warn us if anyone got too near the house. Still, my heart was thumping painfully in my chest.

I'd opened my mouth to repeat my earlier question about the strange tinkling noises when James's phone rang.

He fished it out of his pocket and looked at the screen. "It's Mary. I asked her to check on some things."

He talked to his friend for several minutes, or rather he listened mostly, saying the occasional "uh-huh" and glancing my way.

Finally he said, "Okay, yeah, that's a good idea. Thanks, Mare. Say, can you see if you can find out anything about a woman he's had living with him lately. All I have is a first name." He looked at me. "Was it Toni or Tami?"

"Toni, with an *i*." I mimicked Phillip's sneer which got a lopsided grin out of James.

He repeated the name to Mary. "No, sorry. I don't have a last name, but I can probably get it. I'll call you back." He disconnected.

"What's a good idea?" I asked.

James held up a finger in a wait gesture and tapped his phone screen a couple of times. "A call came in while I was on with Mary. It was Sam."

He held the phone out so we could both hear the message coming through the speaker. "Got us on Judge Petry's schedule for four-thirty today. Meet y'all at the courthouse."

"Thank God," James said.

My heart rate kicked up another notch. I still wasn't sure about this restraining order idea. "What if Greg hasn't found me yet? What if he isn't even looking? Then the restraining order will stir him up, and tell him where I am."

James turned to me with a you've-got-to-be-kidding look on his face. Then his expression softened and he shook his head a little. "I know it's Greg out there." He pointed to the gun on the pillow. "And I'm real glad you gave me lessons on how to use that."

I felt the blood drain from my cheeks at the thought of a shootout between Greg and James. Yes, James was good at hitting tin cans, but Greg was a hunter, had been all his life. He was as comfortable with a gun as he was with a fork and spoon.

James patted my hand. "Hopefully it won't come to that." He was developing the ability to read my mind, which was two parts endearing and one part annoying.

"I'm not going back to DC tonight," he added.

"What about your early audition tomorrow?"

"I'll call my agent in a little bit, tell him I'm unavailable, for the next week at least."

My throat tightened. "Oh, James."

He trapped my hand between both of his. "You're more important than any dumb play. And I wouldn't be able to concentrate. I'd probably flub my lines."

I nodded, my throat and chest still tight with guilt.

"I'm going to go change to meet the judge." He let go of my hand and pushed himself up off the sofa. "Then I'll pull the Mustang up in front of your house, to minimize your exposure when you and Phillip get in."

"Does he have to go?" I wanted to spare my son from hearing Sam describe the abuse that would justify the restraining order, even though Phillip had witnessed some of that abuse firsthand.

"Yes." James stared down at me, warmth and pain in his eyes. "It's not safe to leave him here."

The unsaid words, *now that Greg has probably found you*, hung in the air.

CHAPTER FOUR

Carrie

The judge, a tall, beefy gentleman with a thatch of white hair, couldn't have been any nicer. He seemed to get my ambivalence about the whole affair.

Except for our party, the courtroom was deserted this late in the day. Sam outlined the gist of the situation, emphasizing that I had fled my husband's house, with little more than the clothes on my back, out of fear for my life. And that I had done so knowing that my husband would never hurt his son.

Sam turned to me. "Do you have anything to add?"

"Your Honor," I said, "I know it looks bad that I left my son behind." Sam had expressed concerns about that issue in his office earlier. "But I knew if I took Phillip that my husband would leave no stone unturned to find us. I was hoping that after a few months, he'd cool off and then we could handle the situation like civilized people."

I'd also been waiting for Phillip's fifteenth birthday at which point the courts back in Connecticut would be more likely to take his wishes into consideration.

"And I didn't want to deprive Phillip of his father or vice versa," I continued. "I only wanted to live long enough..." I choked on the words, "...to see him grown."

The judge lowered his chin to look at Phillip over his reading glasses. "But the boy didn't wait. He followed you. Was your mother's assumption about your father's inability to hurt you incorrect, son?"

The double negative seemed to confuse Phillip for a moment. Then he said, "No, Dad didn't hurt me, but he got really weird after Mom left. He drank a lot, more than usual. And he moved this woman into the house, said I was to call her Mom now."

He gave me a nervous glance, licked his lips. "Then he started whaling on her... Toni, the woman. Like he had on Mom."

My heart constricted in my chest. He hadn't told us that part before. For a fleeting moment, I wondered what else he hadn't told me.

The judge's voice dragged me away from my thoughts.

"I'm granting the protective order." He wrote on the paper in front of him while he continued, "Gregory Peterson is restrained from coming within one hundred feet of Carolyn Peterson when out in public or within that distance from her property line."

"Your Honor," Sam said, "could we include Mr. Fitzgerald's property in that?" He gestured toward James. "He lives next door."

The judge lowered his chin again and peered over his glasses at Sam. "Why?" His tone was a bit clipped.

"He has befriended Mrs. Peterson and their concern is that Mr. Peterson will react with jealousy to their friendship and may attack Mr. Fitzgerald."

The judge sat back and stared at me and James for a long moment. I tried hard to look innocent and sweet, rather than the Jezebel I imagined he was thinking I was.

"So be it." He tapped his pen against the bench. "I'm granting temporary custody to Mrs. Peterson, pending a hearing to be set at a later date. Call my clerk tomorrow, Sam, and get that hearing on the schedule."

"Yes, Your Honor." Sam broke out a big grin.

The judge pursed his lips and shook his head slightly, but there was a twinkle in his eye.

James

Sam had whispered the bad news to me on the way out of the courthouse. The courts were backed up. A more definitive custody hearing probably wouldn't happen for at least three months.

I groaned inside. Greg Peterson might or might not take a temporary custody order seriously. But I managed to maintain a positive front with Carrie and Phillip.

I decided to stop by the sheriff's office on our way out of town, even though it was now quarter after five.

Carrie looked wiped out so I suggested she and Phillip stay in the car.

The sheriff was gone for the day but Deputy William Harris was on duty. Bill and I had a sketchy history, since he'd been convinced at one point that I'd killed Annaleise. But we'd been on decent terms since I'd been exonerated. Friendly even.

He was a good ole boy. We had little in common. And yet we had hit it off, once he'd gotten over suspecting me of murder. He was divorced with no kids and I figured he was lonely. We'd had lunch a few times and had gone fishing once. I'd loved the serenity of being out on the water, but I was a lousy fisherman. He, on the other hand, had hauled in several decent-sized perch.

As much as I'd distrusted women all my life, I'd had my friendship with Annaleise to temper that some. My distrust of men had been more complete, thanks to my stepfather. But Bill Harris's overtures of friendship had begun to break through my defenses, at least a little.

I filled Bill in on the situation with Greg Peterson as succinctly as possible, including that we'd seen a suspicious light up by the woods that morning.

He was nodding as I finished. "I always thought there was somethin' odd 'bout that gal. She don't hardly ever come to town. I'll send a patrol by every hour or so." He tilted his head toward his desk. "I'm on 'til midnight, and I'll tell the night shift what's happenin'. Give a holler if you need us."

I thanked him and made my exit. I wondered who else in town had concluded that there was "something odd" about Carrie because she stayed to herself. This was a borderline sin in a small town.

Carrie was right. If Greg hadn't already found us, the return address on the papers would give him Paxtonburg, Virginia. And there would be plenty of people who'd think of Carrie first when he asked about strange women who'd moved here recently.

I wanted to curse Phillip, but when I walked outside and saw him and his mother in the car, I couldn't. Carrie had reached through between the front seats and was holding his hand.

I knocked on the driver's window and Carrie unlocked the door. I climbed in and smiled at the boy. "How soon do you turn sixteen?"

"Fourteen months and two weeks."

I stifled a chuckle. *But who's counting?*

"I'll teach you to drive the Mustang when the time comes, but you gotta promise not to bang it up."

Phillip grinned at me. "Yes, sir!"

I caught Carrie's gaze in the rearview mirror as I put the car in gear. Her eyes were wide, questioning.

Granted we hadn't talked about the future yet—we'd been taking it slow, both of us more than a little gun shy—but hadn't my performance this morning convinced her of my commitment? And *slow* didn't really feel like an option anymore.

I smiled at her in the mirror. After a second, she smiled back. Butterflies quivered in my stomach even as my chest warmed.

Back at the house, I called my agent while Carrie made dinner.

Charlie Berg spluttered and fumed but he finally got it that I would be unavailable to audition for new parts for a while. "I just hope it isn't too long. You know people in this business have short memories. They'll be saying 'James who?'"

As final shots went, it was shaky. "It's your job to remind them of who I am when the time comes," I said and disconnected.

But the man was right. I couldn't afford to stay out of circulation for too long. I only had a few more years in which I would be able to land leading-man roles.

I did have a trust fund from my stepfather and mother. But it wasn't enough to live off of indefinitely. I'd hoped to have more in savings by now, to carry me through the slow years until I would be mature enough to play the distinguished older gentleman roles—the main character's father or grandfather or the domineering boss/dastardly lord/mafia don villains. But now it looked like I'd be dipping into those savings, instead of adding to them.

Carrie pulled me out of my thoughts with a call to dinner.

She was pale and shaky when I went into the kitchen, but she made a valiant effort to appear normal throughout the meal. It was all I could do to keep from asking her what was wrong, but I figured she didn't want to talk about it in front of the boy.

After he'd polished off two servings, he stood to clear the table. "I'll wash up, Mom."

"Thanks," I said, "but I'll get it. You go relax. It's been a long day."

Carrie and I cleared the table in silence, waiting for the crashing sounds of a computer game in progress before speaking.

"What?" I said.

She held out her phone, a disposable one—theoretically untraceable. On the screen were four words.

I will get you.

CHAPTER FIVE

James

I took the phone from her trembling hand. My heart pounded—one part anger, one part fear. *My God, he's definitely found us!*

Or at least he'd somehow gotten her phone number.

Pausing only a moment to reflect on the consequences of what I was about to do, I typed in, *I have a restraining order. 100 feet from me and my house.*

Holding up the phone for Carrie to see, I hit *send*.

Her eyebrows flew up. She snatched the phone away from me and stepped back. "Why'd you do that?"

My heart rate kicked up a couple more notches. I'd considered the consequences in terms of her husband, but not her reaction. I'd assumed she'd be pleased. My gut twisted.

"A restraining order doesn't do any good," I tried to keep the annoyance out of my voice, "if he doesn't know it exists."

She stared at me, her lips clamped into a thin line. Then she broke eye contact, glanced around the room. "I suppose."

She shivered and my insides melted into a dark, seething pool of fear and regret.

I closed the distance between us, gathered her into my arms. "You've got to stand strong."

She went rigid for a few seconds, then relaxed against my chest. "I'm afraid strength isn't one of my virtues," she said into my shoulder.

I took her by the forearms and held her away from me so I could look into her face. "That's bull! You've got all kinds of strength. You're a survivor."

She rolled her eyes.

My stomach quivered as I struggled with how to support, bolster her. "I know the term gets overused these days, but it's valid here. You survived fifteen years with a batterer, and you found the strength to get away from him."

She shrugged, then nodded, but I didn't think I'd convinced her.

"We never finished our talk about the wind chimes," she said.

I suspected she was just trying to change the subject, but I wasn't up for that particular topic right now. It had a been a long, rough day, for both of us.

"Some other time." I squeezed her arms gently and let go of her. "I want to check the window locks. I'm going to sleep on the sofa tonight."

I walked away before she had a chance to respond.

Carrie

I laid the phone on the counter while I finished cleaning up, waiting with a stuttering heart for the ping that would announce an incoming text.

Nothing happened.

Why wasn't Greg firing back some threat?

The murmur of voices coming from the study, Phillip's temporary room. If and when the dust settled, I'd find a bed and dresser somewhere and move him to one of the empty bedrooms upstairs.

If Greg doesn't kill me. I shuddered.

James walked past the kitchen doorway on his way to the living room. He had his cell phone to his ear. "Toni Hamilton... Oh, you pursued that..." He glanced my way. His voice faded to murmuring as he moved away.

I dried my hands and followed him into the living room.

He glanced at me, worry in his eyes. "Okay, thanks, Mare. You're a godsend."

"What did Mary have to say?" I struggled for a normal tone, hoped I'd achieved it.

If I hadn't, he gave no sign. "Toni with an *i* is no longer at your... Greg's house. Nobody's there."

"How did she find that out if she didn't have the woman's last name yet?"

"She, uh, found it by other means. But what is more interesting is that the woman works for a cell phone company."

I processed that for a moment. "So you think she knows how to track a phone, even a disposable one?"

"Mary thinks so. The cellular company would be able to find out what numbers were transmitted via a given cell tower at a given time. Have you and Phillip called each other at all?"

My chest tightened. "Yes, last night. I let Ginger out and she didn't come back when I called. The floodlights don't extend quite as far as the limits of her fence. Phillip went out to get her. When they didn't come back right away, I got nervous and called his phone."

"Where were they?"

"Ginger had gotten her collar caught on a fallen branch along the side of the house. It took him a couple minutes to get her free."

James nodded, frowning. "Mary said that if someone was monitoring towers in the area for Phillip's number and picked up whatever other numbers were also passing through that tower at the time–"

"They could figure out by process of elimination which one was the supposedly untraceable one." I blew out air. Another thought struck me. "But why is this woman helping Greg find me? Wouldn't that be the last thing she'd want?"

Then I answered my own question. *He probably told her he needed to get rid of me so he could marry her.*

James's movements were stiff as he stepped toward me, his eyes not quite meeting mine.

"What aren't you telling me?" I demanded.

He said nothing, pocketed his cell, then rubbed his hand on his jeans-clad thigh.

My stomach clenched. "James?" The firmness in my voice surprised me. It was the voice I'd used when Phillip was little, to get him to obey me—before the abuse had escalated and my fear of Greg had drained away my will.

"Mary hired a private investigator. I told her to." James sighed. "Rather, she suggested it and I said yes. Nobody's been at your house for several days now, but the P.I. found out Toni's last name by interviewing the neighbors, and Mary checked her out from there."

A twinge of fear and shame tightened my throat and heated my cheeks—an echo of the belief that at all costs I had to keep the neighbors from finding out what was going on, the knee-jerk need to keep up appearances that we had the perfect family, the perfect life that Greg demanded.

Who do you think called the cops when the yelling got loud enough?

I shook my head. We hadn't fooled those neighbors, and their opinions didn't matter now anyway. I was never going back to that house.

"The P.I. also talked to Greg's business partner," James was saying, "Allen Torenson. He asked him where Greg was but the guy got cagey. Wouldn't give him a straight answer."

"Hmm, I guess underneath he still feels loyal to Greg."

James raised an eyebrow. "Oh?"

"Greg and Allen had been good friends, until they went into business together about ten years ago. They've never seen eye to eye on how things should be run. Allen has been wanting to buy Greg out for a while now."

"Well, the detective's checking the partner out some more. He's hoping the guy will give him a lead on where Greg is."

"Okay," I said. "That was probably a good idea, hiring the P.I., but I'm paying him."

"I hired him." His tone was firm, slightly angry. "I'm paying his bill."

My hands went to my hips. "James."

He glared at me for a second, then his face softened. He lifted my right hand from my hip and brought it to his lips, kissing the knuckles. "I'm paying," he said softly.

I ignored the tingling sensations running up my arm. Recalling his repeated insistence this morning that we were in this together, I said, "How about this, we'll split it?"

He smiled, his teeth flashing white in his handsome face.

And I nearly swooned. Sometimes I feel like a schoolgirl, with a crush on my favorite actor.

And maybe he's acting now.

Where had that come from? Why would he be *acting* like he cared? He'd put his career on hold, was putting his life on the line.

But still the seed of niggling doubt had been planted.

"Why don't you go on to bed?" James was saying. "Ginger will cover the back door and I'll sleep out in the living room. Between us and the alarm, nobody's getting anywhere near you or Phillip tonight."

"Okay." I reluctantly slid my hand from his. "I'll get you a blanket and pillow."

I went to bed as James had suggested, but sleep was elusive. Staring at the ceiling, my body craving his warmth beside me, the seed sent little tendrils out to wrap around my brain cells.

Greg had been protective, and oh so charming, when I'd first met him. He couldn't wait to replace the father who had died and the older brother who'd abandoned me, to sweep in and take me away from my horrible dysfunctional mother.

And then he'd joined forces with that mother once we were married, insisted we visit her regularly as a good daughter and son-in-law should. And they'd ganged up on me, taking turns putting me down, pointing out my deficiencies as a wife, daughter, mother.

Tears leaked from the corners of my eyes. I fought back the urge to sob.

Perhaps I should let myself cry, get the hurt out. Wasn't that what the shrinks said you should do?

But it felt like giving in—to the past, to Greg, to my mother. I swallowed hard, rolled over, beat my pillow into a thick clump under my cheek.

Gritting my teeth, I prayed for sleep.

My prayers went unanswered until a faint light turned the bedroom curtains to a pale beige. My body relaxed. I had once again survived the night.

I fell into a deep sleep.

James

Ignoring the blanket and pillow Carrie had brought me, I sat up on the sofa, the pistol in my lap, my eyes on the front door.

I dozed occasionally, until my head would fall forward and wake me. I'd readjust my position, then stare at the small, reassuring light on the alarm box by the door that said the system was on and all was well.

I didn't know what to do with my brain.

Usually, if I couldn't sleep, I thought about Carrie. How her soft body melded against mine when we made love. How her eyes shone with warmth when she looked at me, how her sweet lips curved into a smile when I said something even slightly funny.

But tonight those thoughts either made my body ache for her or scared the crap out of me. What if Greg got past me somehow? Maybe I should be in her bedroom, sitting in a chair watching over her.

I shook my head. No. If I were in the bedroom, I wouldn't be able to resist the temptation to crawl into bed with her.

Normally when I was away from Carrie, it was because I was in DC, staying at my apartment during rehearsals or the run of a play. At those times, I usually distracted myself from my longing for her by thinking about my acting.

I loved to act. Nothing had ever made my blood stir quite like it. That is, until I met Carrie.

But tonight, thoughts of my work were also frustrating. Who knew when I would be free to leave Carrie for even an instant?

Could I take her back with me to DC? Her and the boy. But they'd have to come to auditions with me, and then to the rehearsals, and to every performance.

And they still might not be safe. I couldn't watch them every minute when I was on stage....

My head jerked up from the arm of the sofa. Pain shot through my neck and partway down my back. One side of my chin was wet with drool.

My cheeks flushed even though I was alone. I sat up.

Ginger barked and I realized that's what had woken me. I jumped up, fumbled the pistol as it almost fell to the floor.

The sound of claws scrambling, more barking. I raced into the kitchen.

Ginger stood on her hind legs, front paws against the edge of the window in the back door, a deep rumbling coming from her throat.

"Shh, good girl," I hissed quietly. "It's okay."

She turned her head to look at me, then returned her stare to the backyard.

I nudged her aside and looked out.

Early dawn light flooded the weedy fields behind our houses. Two squirrels played tag in the middle of Carrie's yard, apparently oblivious to Ginger's strenuous objections to their presence.

I scanned the scene once, twice. Reassured that the squirrels were the only intruders, I headed back toward the living room.

Carrie came down the stairs, her pink terrycloth robe hastily wrapped around her, her face slack from having been jolted from a deep sleep. Eyes wide, she whispered, "Greg?"

"It's okay," I said quietly. "Just squirrels."

Carrie gave Ginger, who'd followed me from the kitchen, a mock glare. Then she crouched down and scratched the dog's ears.

I continued to the front of the house, peered out the front window. I turned off the alarm and opened the front door. Gun in hand, I stepped out on the porch.

Ginger raced past me, headed for the front field.

The sun rising behind the house cast the porch in shadow. I hoped I was hidden enough to be a poor target for anyone lurking in the woods up by the road. I walked from one end of the porch to the other, peeked around the corners and scanned the side yards.

Nothing. I moved back to the door, slid my gaze back and forth over the woods, my garage, our cars in the driveways, the lawn.

I called Ginger back inside and locked the door. Resetting the alarm, I followed my nose to the kitchen.

Carrie was getting out the makings of breakfast, the coffee already dribbling into the carafe of her coffee maker.

How long can we live like this?

CHAPTER SIX

Carrie

I stared longingly out the kitchen window at my garden. Two days had gone by, with nothing happening. How long could we stay in the house, under siege, when we didn't even know if the enemy was out there?

Until I could file for divorce and get final custody of Phillip? That was months away. And would that keep Greg from coming after me, just because we were no longer legally married?

On the other hand, what if Greg hadn't even followed Phillip? What if he was happy with this Toni woman and had declared good riddance regarding his son?

That *I'll get you* text, maybe he'd sent it just to mess with my head.

"What's the matter?" James's voice startled me out of my reverie.

"I was going to sow some vegetable seeds this weekend. If I don't get them in soon..." It might already be too late. I was used to Connecticut's planting schedule, not northern Virginia's.

James stepped up beside me and looked out the window. "It's too dangerous." His voice was regretful. "He could be out there." He waved his hand toward the overgrown field beyond my backyard.

At the far end of that field was a small lake where people liked to fish, where Ginger and I had taken sack lunches to James and Bill Harris, one day a few weeks ago. As nerve-racking as the last few months had been, that freedom to move around, with Ginger as my early warning system, felt like heaven in retrospect.

My body was heavy, my muscles tight. I knew this feeling too well—dread like a brick in my stomach, droves of butterflies anxiously dancing in my chest.

Get it over with!

The anticipation, the not knowing when, became harder to bear than the beating itself. At times like this, I'd done something on purpose to aggravate Greg, so we could get past the horrible anticipation, past the beating, and move on to a more pleasant phase—when, if not remorseful, he was at least somewhat kind to me.

"Might flush him out," I said.

"Or he could shoot you."

"He won't." My voice conveyed more conviction than I felt. "If he's mad enough to kill me, he'd want to do it up close, see the fear in my eyes."

I sensed James stiffening beside me. "It is a nice day," he said carefully.

I sighed. "I don't really care that much about the gardening, but... I'd like to force his hand. Find out if he *is* here, and if so where things stand."

James rubbed the back of his neck and blew out air. He turned to me. "Phillip and I will stand guard–"

The butterflies doubled their efforts. "No, Phillip stays inside. I don't want him getting caught in the crossfire." *Emotionally or physically*, I added mentally.

James cocked his head, giving that some thought. "Okay, but you yell bloody murder at the first sign of trouble."

I would have preferred a different choice of words but I nodded.

"I'm going to tie Ginger to a post on the front porch." His voice was grim. "If he comes from that direction, she'll let us know."

I nodded again and pulled a light jacket off its peg by the door, shoving my phone into its pocket.

James took Ginger's leash from another peg. She jumped around in excitement.

Phillip came into the kitchen. "What's going on?"

James filled him in on the plan to flush his father out, if he was indeed watching the house.

Meanwhile, my brain was churning out worst-case scenarios—Greg shooting at me and missing, the bullet going through a window and hitting my son.

James took the dog out to the porch.

I turned to Phillip. "You stay in the house, no matter what. Stay in the living room. Keep an eye on Ginger."

He nodded, his normally smooth face pinched with anxiety. "You really think Dad's out there?"

I didn't respond, unwilling to say the truth out loud, and unwilling to lie to my son.

He ducked his head. "I'm sorry." He sounded a little choked up. "I didn't mean to lead him here."

A denial that he had would insult his intelligence. "I know. But he probably would've found me eventually." I paused, the brick of dread growing in my stomach. "Maybe we shouldn't do this."

He shook his head. "No, if he's out there, waiting for a chance to hurt you... Better to lure him out, and try to get him to see reason."

I reached out and ruffled his hair. "How'd I get so lucky and get such a smart kid?" *And brave*, I thought but didn't say.

He gave me a lopsided grin and headed for the front of the house, passing James in the kitchen doorway.

When Phillip was out of earshot, I whispered, "Where's the gun?"

James patted the bulky bulge in his jacket pocket. "I'll keep an eye on the sides and back of the house."

I felt queasy. I opened my mouth to ask for the pistol. An image popped up in my head, of Greg getting the drop on me while I was absorbed in what I was doing—and getting the gun away from me. I shuddered. *Is this worth it?* For a moment, panic overwhelmed—a pure instinctual fear of dying.

I glanced at James. *We can't go on like this.* Besides the emotional toll of waiting, not knowing, he had a career he needed to get back to.

I squared my shoulders. "Okay, let's do it."

James did a perimeter check and then escorted me to my garden shed. I unlocked the padlock and he gestured for me to step back.

Suddenly I wanted to laugh out loud. I felt trapped in a grade B movie, with people imagining enemies in ridiculous places. I remembered the text from Greg, and my desire to giggle faded.

How should I interpret the *I'll get you* message if he didn't show today? Did he mean get me legally? Take Phillip away from me, leave me without a dime. He'd threatened those outcomes often enough, if I ever dared to leave him.

I didn't care about the money, but I couldn't bear the thought of losing custody of Phillip, now that I had him back with me. My stomach twisted.

James had determined that my shed was free of intruders. I gathered my tools and supplies—garden trowel, gloves, bag of compost, and seed packets.

My body tense, I pulled the few weeds that had sprung up and began to prepare the soil, breaking up clumps of clay, which was much more common here than in Connecticut, and working in the compost. Soon the rhythm of the tasks had soothed me some. I scattered lettuce seeds over the loose soil and sprinkled a thin layer of compost on top.

I sat back on my heels and scanned my surroundings. Nothing moved but a squirrel digging for acorns farther down the yard. The fear had subsided a bit, had become background anxiety. I scooted over and started on the soil for the carrots.

I missed the improvised greenhouse I'd created with heavy plastic on the back porch of the Connecticut house. It had allowed me to start tomato and pepper seeds during the early spring and then transfer the plants outside once the hard freezes were done.

It was the only thing I missed about that house. Greg had controlled how it was decorated, what appliances we would buy. I'd had little say in anything except the garden.

I glanced up at my house. *It* felt like home, now that Phillip was here.

James periodically rounded a corner of the house, moved across the back in the shadows under the eaves, and disappeared around the other side. He didn't speak, for which I was grateful. I was in the zone, even enjoying the escape that I knew would be short-lived.

At some point, wind chimes sounded. I was so used to them, they barely registered.

I spread the last of the carrot seeds and gently dusted soil over them, then struggled to my feet, my shoulders and back aching with a pleasant feeling of accomplishment.

Wind chimes clattered. I whirled around.

"Hello, Carolyn."

CHAPTER SEVEN

Carrie

Greg's voice was the pleasant baritone of the man I'd fallen in love with.

I cringed, my heart pounding, my knees weak. I'd forgotten how big he was.

"Where'd you come from?" I managed to get out.

He waved toward the field behind us, his camouflage hunting jacket falling open to reveal a muddy tee-shirt and dark green cargo pants. "Belly-crawled through the weeds. Not all that different from basic training."

Anger flared in my chest, even as my own belly twisted into a knot. He'd been in the National Guard for less than two years when multiple drunk and disorderlies and a couple of AWOLs earned him a bad conduct discharge, but he loved to act like the veteran that he wasn't.

He took a step toward me, grinning.

My heart bounced frantically off the walls of my chest. My feet were frozen to the ground.

"I stopped moving when I saw your boyfriend stick his head out." His grin widened. "Could've taken him out more than once."

My insides quivered like jello.

Greg's face shifted to menacing, eyes narrowed, lips in a flat line. "Where's my son?"

I felt the urge to explain, to point out that Phillip had found me of his own free will. But I knew I had less than a minute before Greg would pounce. I had to make every word count.

"I don't want to keep him from you. We'll work out a schedule—"

"I want my son," he growled. "Now! You don't care about him. You left him."

Those words would have squeezed my heart if I hadn't been so focused on survival. I measured the distance between us. Too far away to use any of the self-defense tactics I'd made a point of learning since last facing off with this man.

Then Greg took several quick steps forward, his big hands reaching for me. One grabbed my hair and gave it a vicious tug. The other closed around my throat. "Where's my son, bitch?" His face moved close to mine, twisted into an ugly sneer. "Give him to me or I'll kill you and that bastard you've been screwing."

I stomped my foot down on the instep of his boot. He flinched and his grip on my neck loosened.

My other knee came up.

I must've closed my eyes. My knee connected with something. A yelp of pain. He let go of my throat.

A gunshot exploded. "Freeze!" James yelled.

My eyes flew open. The pistol in James's hand was pointed at the sky.

My brain seemed to have detached itself from the horror of the situation. It had happened before, during the worst of the beatings. I noted calmly that I'd overlooked the gun safety lecture about what goes up must come down. But it was unlikely out here in the country that anything alive would be hit by his descending bullet.

Greg was on his knees, holding his crotch and rocking back and forth.

In the next second, James was behind him, the barrel of the pistol two inches from his head.

I gasped, snapping back into the reality of the moment. *Dear Lord, no!*

Fortunately, James had more self-control than I'd given him credit for. He glanced up at me. "Where'd you learn that?"

My ears still ringing from the gunshot, I read his lips more than heard the words. "Self-defense class I took," I said, breathing heavily, "in one of the towns I stayed in for a while."

I pulled out my phone.

The back door flew open. "Go back inside," I yelled at Phillip, but he stayed in the doorway.

My fingers shook slightly as I dialed 911. I filled the dispatcher in as succinctly as possible.

"Are y'all in immediate danger?" the woman said.

"No. We've got things under control for now."

"I'll get somebody to ya quick as I can."

My tense muscles relaxed slightly. "Thank you." I disconnected.

James had been glancing at me while keeping his gun trained on Greg, who was still groaning on his knees. "Get up!" he said now.

Greg staggered to his feet.

"Phillip," James called out. "Step back, please."

My jaw dropped. "What are you doing?"

"They'll be awhile getting here. We might as well get comfortable." His words sounded casual but his tone was anything but. "Peterson, go inside and sit at the kitchen table. Keep your hands where I can see them."

As James followed Greg inside, he gestured for me to follow also.

Feeling a bit nauseous, I complied.

James pointed to the kitchen chairs on the opposite side of the table from where Greg now sat, his jacket puffing out around him making him look even bigger, his ham-like fists on the tabletop.

Phillip sat down. In need of a few moments to calm myself down, I continued through the room and retrieved Ginger from the porch. She growled as I led her past the kitchen doorway. I closed her in the study.

When I returned to the kitchen, the men were silent. James leaned against the counter, the pistol aimed in Greg's direction. He nodded to me, and I pulled a chair back out of Greg's reach and sat down.

"Okay, here's the deal," James said to Greg. "Your son has chosen to live with his mother. So here are your options." He tapped the index finger of his left hand against the gun. "One, I shoot you now before the deputy, who happens to be a friend of mine, gets here. Then I drag you outside the door and claim I shot you while you were trying to break in."

James's middle finger tapped the gun. "Two, you go back home and accept the custody arrangement and visitation schedule the Virginia courts dictate. Three, you contest Carrie's case and we duke it out in front of a judge."

He bent at the waist, thrust his face down closer to Greg's. "But, bottom line, you act like a civilized human being and accept *some* legal settlement made by a court of law, or I blow you away right now!"

James leaned back against the counter. "So what'll it be," his tone was casual, "a civilized settlement or sure death?"

My heart had been pounding, my mind debating James's sanity, but now I smiled a little. My chest filled with a strange feeling. After a second or two, I decided it was a good feeling.

Greg's mouth curled in a sneer, but his eyes registered something I'd never seen there before.

Fear?

"And what happens if I agree to let the courts settle it?" His tone was condescending, belittling.

But it failed to intimidate me this time. Some part of my brain registered it as the desperate attempt at bravado that it was.

"You walk out of here alive," James said in a matter-of-fact voice, "and you get to see your son occasionally." He leaned forward again. "And if you don't agree to that, I blow your brains out."

For a second the mask crumbled and Greg's whole face registered fear. Then he squared his shoulders. "Sure, okay. We let the courts decide."

I heard Phillip blow out air. "I'll come see you this summer, Dad." The relief in his voice was palpable.

My heart lightened some. This was the right thing to do. But I wasn't quite ready to relax yet.

Greg glanced at his son, then back at James, who was now standing straight, his pistol aimed at Greg's head.

"I know you're armed," James said. "Where's your gun?"

Greg sat perfectly still for a couple of seconds. Then he pointed to the pocket of his hunting jacket.

"Two fingers, pull it out slowly." James gestured slightly up and down with his gun. "Put it on the table and shove it over to Phillip."

Another beat of stillness. Greg complied, laying his .380 on the table and pushing it with two fingers over to our son.

I realized I was digging my fingernails into my palms and willed my hands to uncurl.

"Empty the bullets, Phillip," James said.

My son picked up the gun and expertly ejected the magazine.

"Stand up and turn out your pockets," James said to Greg.

With a sneer, he complied. A pair of gloves fell out of one coat pocket. Two power bars from the other.

"Pants."

A beat of hesitation, then Greg turned out his pants' pockets. A box of bullets clunked to the floor.

Sirens in the distance. James's gaze cut sideways to Phillip, then back to Greg. "Get them."

Phillip stood and scurried over, picked up the box. He moved quickly back to stand beside my chair.

I took his hand. It was clammy.

"Sit," James commanded, waggling the gun at Greg, who resumed his seat.

The sirens were getting closer. We sat, or in James's case, stood, in uncomfortable silence.

The siren squealed to a stop. A few seconds later, the doorbell rang.

Muffled barking from the study.

"Get the door, Phillip," James said.

I let go of my son's hand. He left the room, and I took the first decent breath in the last half hour.

A few seconds later, Bill Harris came through the kitchen doorway, his hand on the butt of his gun in its holster. With a glance, he took in the scene.

"You wanna press charges, Ms. Peterson?"

"For what?" Greg said with another sneer.

James looked at me, eyebrows arched, as he pocketed his gun.

That threw me. Was he trying to tell me something?

"She got a restraining order," Phillip said from behind the deputy.

Greg smirked at me. "I can't believe you actually got up the nerve."

"You didn't know she had the order?" Bill Harris stood with legs spread, one hand still resting on his holstered gun, the other on his silver belt buckle—a deer leaping through the woods. I somehow doubted it was part of the standard sheriff's department uniform.

Greg shook his head. "I had no idea, Officer."

Yeah, right. It was typical Greg behavior. When the law showed up, he was all innocence and light.

"It's *Deputy*," Harris said, "You–"

"He knew," I interrupted. "We texted him."

Greg glared at me, shaking his head again. "Don't know what you're talking about."

"You promise not to violate the order again?" Harris said.

Greg nodded.

"Then get outta here."

I opened my mouth to protest. "He grabbed–"

"What about my gun?" Greg said loudly, drowning me out.

"Don't push it," Harris replied.

James had stepped over beside me. He discreetly took my hand, down by my side, and squeezed it.

Greg rose from the table.

I opened my mouth again. "He tried to cho–"

Greg hitched up his belt and the words froze in my throat. I struggled not to cringe back, my mind flooding with the times he'd unbuckled that belt and beat me with it.

James tightened his grip on my hand.

"Do what he says, Dad," Phillip begged. "Please!"

Again, Greg's expression surprised me, left me speechless. His face filled with pain and confusion.

After a pause, he shrugged and walked toward the back door.

Once there, he turned. He stared at Phillip, then at me, his lips clenched tight. His cheeks reddened.

"Dad, go!" Phillip said. "I'll see you in June."

Greg turned, opened the kitchen door, and walked out of my house.

Air whooshed out of my lungs, although I'd have been happier if he'd been going to jail.

Harris gave us a small salute, pivoted and headed for the front door.

I let him find his own way out.

CHAPTER EIGHT

James

My insides quaking some, I hustled over and locked the back door behind my lover's abusive husband.

When I turned, Carrie was standing, hands on her hips. "Why didn't you want me to press charges?"

My thoughts were a bit jumbled, and her accusatory question wasn't helping. Something about Bill Harris's reaction bothered me, but I couldn't put my finger on why. "What do you mean?"

"All the eyebrow arching and hand squeezing," she said.

I glanced at Phillip. His expression was hard to read. I cut him some slack. This couldn't be easy for him, caught in the middle.

"I didn't necessarily *not* want you to press charges." I wasn't sure I'd wanted her to either. "I was going on instinct," I continued, "trying to show Greg that I was tougher than him, without rubbing his face in it too much."

"Yeah, okay, that's why you said what you did to him." She sounded exasperated. "But why not have him arrested? He attacked me!"

Her tone annoyed me. "Look, I was trying to be supportive. And I didn't stop you from pressing charges. Besides, having him arrested could have gone either way. It might have increased the chances that he'd leave us alone, or it could have pissed him off even more."

To my surprise, Carrie deflated.

She nodded and sank back down at the kitchen table. "I think I've read every self-help book ever written about domestic violence. One of the things I learned was that Greg's a bully. And bullies are actually scared inside. They use bullying to compensate for their insecurities. And when confronted, as you say, they can go either way."

I watched Phillip out of the corner of my eye. His mouth was hanging open. But then he slowly nodded, acknowledging his mother's portrayal of his father.

I turned to him. "Would you mind going out and cleaning up from your mother's gardening? I'll watch from the window. If I rap on it, get inside quick."

Phillip hesitated, then headed for the kitchen door.

"The seeds need watering," Carrie said. "Set the hose nozzle on low pressure, just a gentle mist."

The boy nodded and went out the door.

I closed and locked it. Standing off to one side of its window, my eyes scanned the weeds in the field beyond where Phillip was dragging out the hose.

"So either we scared him off," I said to Carrie over my shoulder, "or he'll hit back even harder."

A low sound, somewhere between a snort and a chuckle. Carrie stepped up behind me. "I did say I wanted to force his hand, didn't I?"

I shifted to the side and wrapped my arm around her shoulders, keeping my body between her and the door. She laid her head against my chest.

My gaze still on Phillip, who was now watering the garden, I dropped a kiss on the top of her hair.

Her dark, luscious, wavy hair. She'd been dyeing it blonde and straightening it when I'd met her, part of her efforts to hide from Greg. Lately, she'd let it grow out and go back to her natural color. The overhead kitchen light caught the red highlights. I stroked its silky softness, my mind flashing to Greg grabbing it and yanking.

"I'm so sorry," I whispered, my throat tight, "that I didn't get there faster, that he was able to hurt you."

"It was only a few seconds." She smiled up at me. "And then you were there, my brave hero."

I snorted. "One of my better performances." But I stopped short of admitting how scared I had been. I didn't want her to go back into get-away-from-James-to-protect-him mode.

We stood side by side, my arm around her, watching her son haul tools and compost into the garden shed.

Inside, my gut twisted. I thought there was a decent chance that Peterson would leave us alone. To be honest, Phillip's words had probably swayed him more than mine. It had been obvious that the boy wanted peace between his parents.

But we had to be prepared for the worst, for retaliation, escalation.

That's when it hit me, what had been bothering me about Bill Harris's reaction. I was pretty sure that Carrie didn't need to press charges to enforce a restraining order. Bill should have arrested Peterson and dragged him off to jail.

If he'd done that, without asking about pressing charges, it would have reinforced that the law was on our side. And it would have been the sheriff's department arresting Greg for breaking the law, not us *getting* him arrested—a big difference psychologically.

Why had Bill taken Greg's word over hers that he didn't know about the restraining order?

Guilt filled my chest. *Why didn't I do more to stand up for her?*

A fist closed around my heart. I'd counted Bill a friend, and he'd seemed sympathetic when I'd talked to him at the sheriff's department on Thursday.

But apparently old-school sexism overrode friendship.

It was a glimpse into the world Carrie had lived in for years, where her word was never quite as good as that of the man who abused her, and law enforcement was less than aggressive about protecting her rights, much less her safety.

Carrie

After Phillip was safely back inside, I cobbled together a dinner of canned soup and grilled cheese sandwiches, using the last of the bread.

As we sat down, I caught James's eye, then glanced at the empty bread wrapper I'd left on the counter.

His lips pressed together and he gave a slight nod. Message received. We were in desperate need of groceries.

We ate in silence. I considered trying to start a conversation, but decided it was best to leave everyone to their own thoughts. It had been a long, tense afternoon.

Now we had to wait and see. Either Greg would leave us alone, or he'd come at us again, perhaps with more vehemence. The consequences of the latter response were obvious, but the former response had its own problems. We wouldn't have any way of knowing if Greg had truly gone away, or was just biding his time, waiting for us to let our guard down.

As I ate, I analyzed Greg's actions and words, a habit developed out of self-preservation over the years of our marriage.

Yes, he'd tried to choke me, but he hadn't drawn his gun, even though he knew James was nearby. He'd threatened to kill us, but he hadn't tried to shoot either of us.

His words had all been about Phillip. Maybe he had given up on dragging me back home. He just wanted his son. Maybe he'd accept visitation. I'd let him have the whole summer and every holiday if that would placate him.

But until we had that custody hearing, we couldn't let our guard down. I wouldn't be surprised if Greg tried to snatch Phillip and take him back to Connecticut by force.

Phillip finished eating and asked to be excused.

"Sure," James said. "I'll get the dishes."

After a few minutes, the now familiar sounds of a video game came from the study.

Another downside to the situation—my son needed to be in school, not spending all his time killing off imaginary aliens. But I couldn't send him to school if his father was still out there. Maybe I could home-school him for the rest of this year.

And what about Phillip's promise to visit his father in June? The hearing wasn't until early July.

I shook my head. I had three months to sort that out.

"Leave the dishes," I said to James, gesturing toward the front of the house. "Let's sit for a while."

I needed a distraction and my curiosity about the wind chimes was now even more aroused. When I'd first heard them, I'd been confused. Then I'd wondered if a window in the attic was loose in its frame and was rattling occasionally. Before I'd gotten around to checking out that theory—getting into the attic required hauling a ladder inside and climbing up through a trap door—I'd gotten used to the sound, and had come to find it almost comforting.

But James's reaction when we'd both heard it had me intrigued, and a little anxious.

As soon as we were settled on the sofa, I turned to James. "No evasions this time," I said in a low voice. "What's the wind chime noise I keep hearing?"

James shifted around to face me. His face was pale and his hand shook a little as he reached up to push an errant clump of dark hair off his forehead.

He drew in a slow breath. "It's Annaleise."

CHAPTER NINE

Carrie

"Wha'?" I shook my head. Had I heard him correctly?

"Her ghost, to be precise," he said, breaking eye contact. His fingers plucked at a threadbare spot on the knee of his jeans.

My mouth was hanging open. I closed it. Had the stress pushed James around the bend?

Struggling to sound calm, I asked, "What makes you think it's her?"

His half shrug was no doubt meant to seem nonchalant, but I noted the stiffness in his muscles. "It's how her laughter sounded, like wind chimes in a breeze."

I really would've thought he was crazy, except I'd heard the sound myself so many times.

Do I believe in ghosts? I wasn't sure. I'd always been so fixated on staying alive in this world, I hadn't given what happens after death much thought.

"But it's not always a happy sound," I pointed out. "Sometimes it's... like a warning, like today. And other times it's sounded almost angry."

James shrugged again and looked up. "Yeah, she uses the sound to convey different things, but she's spoken to me on occasion too."

I resisted rolling my eyes, since he was now watching me intently. "And said what?"

"*Look out*, or *wake up*. She can move objects too. That day... a statue flew across the room. And she was the one who knocked the bookcase over."

That day that we'd sworn never to talk about, lest we forget ourselves in public and be overheard by someone. The day we'd killed Annaleise's and her husband's murderer.

"You sure he didn't bump the bookcase when he fell down?"

James shook his head. "He wasn't that close to it." He turned and glanced back over his shoulder, in the direction of the hallway from which faint sounds of battle emanated. "And we should stop talking about this now."

"The ghost?"

"No, that day." He shifted around again on the sofa to face me. "I know it's hard to believe, but Annaleise has warned me several times about things. Sometimes with words, but more often with the wind chimes sound. I guess it's easier for her to laugh than to talk."

My eyebrows went up. I'd never really considered how ghosts communicated. Then I shook my head, my brain resisting the illogic of all this.

I couldn't help myself. The mother in me reached out and felt his forehead.

He chuckled nervously. "I'm not feverish and I'm not delusional." He turned his head toward the empty living room. "Help me out here, Annaleise."

The wind chimes tinkled on cue.

I flopped back against the sofa, my heart pounding some, but whether from excitement or fear, I couldn't say. Goose bumps pebbled my arms. "So we have our own resident ghost. Why didn't you tell me sooner?"

"I didn't realize you could hear her." He paused. "And I thought you'd react the way you have, or worse."

I glanced his way. Worry clouded his eyes.

Concern for him pushed aside my own confused feelings. "I wouldn't have left you." Taking his hand, I gave it a squeeze. "Maybe had you committed though," I added with a small grin.

He returned my grin, a little lopsided at first. But it settled into a more natural smile as the anxiety faded from his eyes.

It was both disconcerting and comforting to think that Annaleise, James's best friend whom I'd never met, was there with us. And I wasn't as surprised as I guess I should've been. Some part of me had always sensed there was a sentient force behind the wind chimes, and that it was benevolent.

We snuggled together on the sofa. Resisting kissing James was hard, but I knew if we started we'd have trouble stopping. It had been several days since we'd slept together, and we weren't used to celibacy.

I would need to have a talk with Phillip soon about my relationship with James.

My eyelids were drooping—it had been a long day.

"My mother's ghost is in my house too."

I jerked upright on the sofa. "What?"

"The violence when Annaleise and Charles were killed, it must have stirred her up. I'd never heard her or felt her presence before that."

"*Two* ghosts?" I croaked out.

He gave me another lopsided smile. "Sometimes they've joined forces to warn me, but mostly Mom is... a warmth that surrounds me."

My mouth gaping, I was giving more serious consideration to a mental health evaluation. But I couldn't decide if it should be for him or for me.

"Look, I know it sounds crazy," James said. "It does to my ears as I'm saying it." He dropped his gaze and plucked at the threads of his jeans again. "I've been wondering lately if I should try to figure out how to, you know, set them free."

A bark of hysterical laughter escaped my throat. "Like go-into-the-light kind of stuff?"

James nodded. "But of course that will have to wait, for now."

I nodded too, feeling a little like I was going along with a crazy person to keep him mollified.

I opened my mouth to say something, although I had no idea what. I yawned instead.

"You should get to bed," James said. "Ginger and I will stand guard down here."

A thought flitted through my brain. Had sleep deprivation addled his mind?

I considered trying to convince him to sleep while I kept guard, but I doubted he'd go along with that. I'd already let on how tired I was.

I stopped to check on Phillip before heading upstairs.

The computer monitor was dark and he was curled up on top of the blanket on the sofa bed, fully clothed. I picked up the throw, crocheted by somebody's mother or grandmother and later relegated to a garage sale, and draped it over him.

James

I jerked awake from my vigil on the sofa. Soft light seeped through the living room curtains. I felt lightheaded and hollow inside. I tried to tell myself it was from lack of sleep, but I knew what it really was.

Fear.

I shouldn't have told her about Mom. It had been one ghost too many.

But they're the reality I deal with.

I snorted at the concept of ghosts and reality in the same thought.

Something stirred at my feet. Ginger raised her head. Sometime during the night, she'd moved from her post in the kitchen. She dropped her head back down on her front paws, apparently not yet ready to call it morning.

I got up carefully, trying not to disturb her, padded in stocking feet to the back door and looked out. No sign of movement in the back field. I made an inside circuit of the house, looking out each window, skipping only Phillip's and Carrie's rooms.

Nothing. The countryside was quiet.

I got a whiff of myself as I lifted an arm to push a curtain back in place. "This is ridiculous," I muttered. I'd been in the same clothes for going on four days, and we were out of food.

I needed to go over to my house and raid the pantry and fridge.

I went back to Carrie's bedroom and then downstairs to the study, gently nudging open each door. The occupants were rounded lumps under their bedding, sleeping soundly.

I went back to the living room, tucked my feet into my loafers, and retrieved my jacket from the other end of the sofa. At the front door, I disarmed the alarm and opened the door partway.

Ginger let out a small, gleeful yelp and took off. I reset the alarm and closed the door behind me.

The dog was running from grass tuft to bush, searching for the perfect spot to pee. My tense muscles relaxed some. I figured she would be barking if anyone was nearby.

As I went down the steps, I noticed a squirrel frozen in place at the end of the porch.

"You better run," I said softly.

The squirrel startled at the sound of my voice and then took off. Ginger spotted him and gave chase, yipping happily.

I chuckled and headed across the lawns.

At my own front door, I paused before unlocking it and took the pistol out of my pocket. I searched the house, letting out my pent-up breath when there was no sign that anyone had been there.

My foraging in the pantry was interrupted by a couple of sharp yelps in the distance. I lifted my head and listened, but the dog didn't bark again.

She's treed the squirrel.

I opened my refrigerator and stared at its pathetic contents.

Carrie

Clattering wind chimes woke me.

I sat up in bed, looked around. The noise sounded like it was coming from downstairs.

I grabbed my robe from the foot of my bed and ran out of my room. "James," I yelled as I dashed down the stairs.

The living room was deserted. I ran into the hallway.

Phillip's door stood ajar. I pushed it open and stuck my head inside. Somewhere during the night he had gotten undressed and crawled under the comforter. I grabbed the knob to pull the door closed but something made me pause. I stared again at the bed, then stepped into the room for a closer look.

Two pillows had been stuffed under the comforter. I yanked them out and tossed them on the floor, frantically calling out Phillip's name.

The wind chimes renewed their clamoring, like an old-fashioned fire bell.

It registered that the curtains on his window had been pushed aside. I stepped farther into the room, trying to process why a block of opaque white would be plastered against the glass.

As I neared it, my heart jumped into my throat. It was a piece of paper, taped to the outside of the window, and on it were words—a bit shaky, but unmistakably Greg's handwriting.

Meet me in the woods. There's something important I need to tell you and then I'll leave you and your mother alone. Dad

My insides twisting into knots, I pivoted and bolted from the room, down the hallway, into the living room. "James! Phillip!" No response.

It registered that the dog hadn't responded to my moving around either. "Ginger?"

Where the hell is everybody?

I flung the front door open. The alarm beeped a warning. I quickly disabled it, then scanned the lawn.

Soft morning light sparkled on the dew of the green expanse before me. It took a moment for the eerie silence to compute. The landscape looked innocent enough, but all was *not* well when no birds chirped.

Then the wind chimes again in the distance, still frantic. The sound was coming from the woods.

"Annaleise?" I whispered.

Phillip! I couldn't tell if the word was my own thought or coming from her.

Run! Stop him!

James

Clean clothes stuffed into a backpack on my shoulder and two cloth sacks of supplies in my hands, I stepped onto Carrie's porch. All was quiet except for a strange clanking sound in the distance. I whistled for the dog.

No response.

I started to call her. "Ging–" died on my lips.

Carrie's front door was standing open.

CHAPTER TEN

Carrie

I raced along the packed dirt trail in the woods. Sticks and small stones poked at my bare feet, but I didn't care. I was intent on following the clattering sound just ahead of me.

My mind flashed to a movie of my youth—Peter Pan. The original black-and-white version, in which Tinkerbell was a small flashing light.

Am I following a fairy? Or a figment of my imagination?

No, the note I'd seen was real and Phillip was gone. I had to trust that Annaleise was leading me to him.

Halfway around a curve, my foot landed on a rock. Sharp pain ripped across my insole.

Leaning against a tree for balance, I lifted my foot to assess the damage. I was gasping for air. As I cradled the foot in my hand, a line of red bubbled along the dirt-smudged skin of my sole.

"Mom?"

My head jerked up and I almost lost my balance.

Phillip stood twenty feet away, a bloody knife in his hand. His father lay at his feet.

———◦———

James

I dropped the bags on the porch and raced through the open door. Frantically, I searched from room to room but the house was empty.

Heart pounding, I yanked out my phone to call the sheriff's department. The screen was dark, and it stayed that way when I pressed the *on* button. The damn thing had run out of juice during the night.

I ran outside, my head swiveling right and left, scanning for any movement. The still lawn sparkled in the sunshine. I raced around the house, took in the empty garden and the long grasses swaying to a soft breeze in the field behind the house. I peeked in the small window of the door to the garden shed, even though a saner part of my mind knew they wouldn't be in there.

Back around front, I scanned the landscape again. It registered that I hadn't seen or heard Ginger for at least twenty minutes. I headed in the direction that I thought her last yelps had come from, the woods beyond the expanse of our lawns.

———◦———

Carrie

Skirting the charred logs of a cold campfire, I knelt at Greg's head and felt around on the side of his neck. His skin was cool. I couldn't find a pulse. I suppressed a shudder and looked up at Phillip.

His eyes wide, mouth hanging open, he shook his head and dropped the knife.

I quickly scanned his clothes—sneakers without socks, sweat pants and a white tee-shirt—what he normally wore to sleep in, minus the sneakers. I didn't see any blood except on his hands, but I'd watched enough TV to know a crime lab would probably find some on the clothing.

For now, I had to get him away from the body.

"Go!" I barked. "Back to the house. Wash your hands. Really good!"

He stood there, staring at me.

"Go, I said!"

He turned and stumbled back along the path I'd come.

I grabbed up the knife and took off in the other direction, deeper into the woods.

James

I tromped through the woods, straining for signs of any human presence other than my own. But all I heard were my own footfalls and the crunching of dried twigs and leaves under my loafers. I caught movement out of the corner of my eye, pivoted, raced toward it. Toward the lighter sky beyond the edge of the woods.

I came out into the sunlight in time to see a woman's form darting across the lawn between me and the house. At first I thought it was one of my ghosts.

But it was Carrie. She wore nothing but a thin nightgown, torn and smudged with dirt. Her feet were bare.

I raced after her.

When I got to the house, the front door was closed but not locked. I tore it open and entered.

I stood in the bare living room. The sound of running water above me signaled that the shower was going in the master bath.

Phillip came down the hall from the study, his feet bare, his hair sticking up in sweaty spikes, as if he'd just gotten up. His jeans and gray sweatshirt seemed fresh. I caught a whiff of the fabric softener Carrie used in her laundry.

But he hadn't been there when I'd searched the house less than a half hour ago.

My head spun. Was this a bad dream? I looked at the sofa, half expecting to see myself sleeping there.

Maybe I *was* losing my mind.

The shower stopped and a toilet flushed above my head.

Had the boy been in the hall bathroom earlier? I hadn't thought to look there. But I would have if the bathroom door had been closed. Had it been? I couldn't remember.

"What's going on?" Phillip said.

"That's what I'd like to know." I went to the bottom of the stairs and yelled, "Carrie!"

Silence for a second, then, "Coming."

A minute or two later, she started down the stairs, slippers on her feet but dressed in jeans and a long-sleeved, man-tailored white shirt. Wet hair dripped into her face. With the towel in her hand she swiped at it while giving me a weak smile. "Good morning."

"Where were you?" I demanded.

She stopped two steps from the bottom and glanced at Phillip.

I hadn't noticed how rigid her body was until it relaxed some. *What the hell?*

"Why, right here, of course," Carrie finally answered me. The corners of her mouth pushed upward, but her eyes were wide and not quite meeting mine.

The lie made my gut twist.

"No you weren't. I searched the house." I pivoted to face Phillip. "Neither of you were in here a little while ago. I went looking for you in the woods."

Phillip and his mother exchanged a glance. "Um, I've been here," the boy said.

"I, uh, went outside," Carrie said, "just briefly, with Ginger."

I turned back and stared up at her, clenching my teeth to keep from calling her a liar. "No, Ginger was with me, and now she's gone."

Something I couldn't read crossed her face. "Um, Phillip, my toilet's stopped up. Could you get the plunger from the hall bathroom?"

He stared at her for a couple of beats, then nodded and headed down the hall.

Carrie descended the last two steps. "I'll explain later," she whispered in a hoarse voice.

I shook my head. Enunciating each word, I said, "What is going on?" I was no longer trying to sit on my anger.

Phillip came back our way, carrying the plunger.

"I, uh..." Carrie had the strangest look on her face. She glanced at her son, then took a deep breath.

"I killed Greg."

CHAPTER ELEVEN

James

It's amazing what parts of an incredible situation the brain latches onto. My first thought was, *That explains the front door being unlocked.* With Greg dead, there was no longer a threat.

Phillip stepped up beside his mother, still carrying that stupid plunger. "No, she didn't. I killed him."

I shook my head at both of them.

"He lured me out into the woods," Phillip said, "with a note on my window. I'll show you." He gestured for me to follow and headed for his room.

Carrie raced after him, plucking at his sweatshirt sleeve. I trailed behind them.

Phillip pointed to a square of white on his window. "I heard a tapping noise and got up to investigate. That's when I found it."

"Is that Greg's handwriting?" I asked.

Carrie nodded.

"Where's his body?" I asked, my mind still reeling.

"Out in the woods," Carrie said. "He'd...um, I killed him with his own knife."

I narrowed my eyes at her, my heart squeezing in my chest. Why did she keep lying to me?

At least I hope she's lying.

My stomach heaved at the thought that she might be a killer, even if her husband did deserve to die. But of course, it most likely was self-defense, as it had been when she'd killed before.

They say it gets easier each time. I shuddered. "Where did you knife him?"

"I told you," she said impatiently, "out in the woods."

"I mean where did you stick the knife?" I turned toward Phillip. "Whichever one of you really killed him, where did you knife him?" My voice was rising despite my best efforts to sound calm.

Carrie recovered first. "I don't remember," she mumbled. "In the stomach, I think."

"He let you get his knife away from him and stick it in his gut?"

She nodded mutely, her face pale.

Phillip piped up. "No, I did that. She found me there standing over him."

My stomach churned. They were both lying.

I snatched the plunger from Phillip's hand. He jumped back, startled.

Disgusted, I stomped up the stairs to the master bathroom to deal with a problem that I *could* handle.

Carrie

"What'd you do with your clothes?" I whispered to Phillip. I'd been a little surprised that he'd thought to change them, but then again, he'd watched plenty of crime shows on TV as well. *Blue Bloods* had been one of our favorites that we'd always tried to watch together.

"Taken care of," he whispered back.

Before I could ask for details, James came down the stairs, some strips of wet cloth dangling from his fingers. "Is this your nightgown? You tried to flush it?"

The anger in his voice made my chest ache. I nodded, unsure that I could trust my voice.

"You went out in nothing but your nightgown?"

"No, I had my robe on."

"Where is it?" he demanded.

"Buried, along with the knife. Deeper in the woods."

He stared at me, then pivoted and went down the hall.

I followed him, trying to figure out what to say. He was so angry. I felt a chasm between us. I desperately needed to reach across it, to touch him. To get him to touch me, to hold me.

My stomach knotted. I needed to get a grip. I had confessed to murder. My life was about to go down the drain. How could I take him down with me?

He ducked into the hall bathroom. The toilet flushed and he came back out. His lips were clamped into a tight line. "There are flecks of red in the sink." His tone was clipped. "Get the bleach."

"You don't need to be involved in this," I blurted out. "You can go home. Pretend this never happened."

I glanced at Phillip. His eyes, now red-rimmed, darted from James to me and back again. His body had deflated, curled in on itself.

It's hit him that his father is dead.

I felt nothing for Greg. Or maybe any grief for him was buried under the fear churning in my belly. My chest was so tight it was hard to breathe.

James glanced at Phillip, then back at me, his eyes narrowed. "I'm not sure I believe that either of you killed him."

Phillip's jaw clenched. He straightened his shoulders. "Why? You don't think I have it in me?"

"No, I don't. Shoot your father if he was about to hurt your mother, maybe, but knife him out in the woods." James shook his head. "I just don't see it."

"I told you I did it," I said, but I could hear the lack of conviction in my own voice.

James looked at me, his face blank. "I wish you hadn't buried the knife."

Phillip hung his head. "I'd touched it. Pulled it out."

Now James nodded, his expression more sympathetic as he turned to my son. "Of course. That would be the natural thing to do. He didn't react when you did that? No new bleeding?"

Phillip face crumpled. A green tinge now shaded his skin. He swallowed hard, visibly trying to pull himself together. "No, his skin was cool."

"So he'd been dead for a while," James said. He was silent for several seconds, staring over our heads. "I think I'll go look for Ginger."

Guilt added to my nausea. I hadn't given the poor dog a thought. "I'll go with you."

"No, we have to act like we don't know Greg is gone." James stared hard into my eyes. "He's still out there, a threat to us. I'll take the gun. You two stay in the house, with the alarm on. Get the bleach and scrub out that sink, and your shower too. I'll pretend to stumble on Greg's body and call the sheriff's department."

"No, James. You should stay out of it. I'll go look for the dog and pretend to find the body."

"Damn it, Carrie!" James yelled.

I jumped.

He leaned in close to my face. "Get this straight, once and for all. We're in this together."

I flinched away.

I heard his teeth grinding. He pivoted and headed for the front door.

"Burn that note on Phillip's window and flush the ashes," he said over his shoulder. "Then start making breakfast and burn some food."

I opened my mouth to say we shouldn't waste any food, then realized that was idiotic. We were no longer prisoners in my house.

———◆———

James

I stepped off Carrie's porch, my insides churning, but I acted nonchalant on the surface, in case someone was out there watching. I whistled and called Ginger's name. It would be a nice touch if I actually found the dog.

I was almost across the mowed field, headed for the spot where I'd seen Carrie coming out of the woods, when something blue flashed through the trees up by the road.

I froze, staring at a line of moving cars, blue lights circling on their roofs. The first one turned into the entrance to our lane.

I took off running for the woods, praying the occupants of those cars hadn't seen me.

I wanted to get to the crime scene before them, in case Carrie or Phillip had left anything behind there.

A few minutes later, I found Ginger. She was sniffing Greg's body, where it was sprawled across a sleeping bag, next to a circle of stones containing some charred logs.

"Get back, girl." I grabbed her collar and hauled her back. Something was caught in the collar's buckle. I pulled it loose. A length of bailing twine, maybe three feet long.

I used it to tie the dog to a sapling a few feet away. "Sit, stay."

The dog dropped her butt to the ground next to the tree and watched me, panting.

Bile rose in my throat as I made myself examine the body. I counted at least a half dozen knife wounds in what had once been the man's abdomen.

I pulled out my phone. My hand was shaking.

Good, lemme see if I can get a little tremor into my voice.

I pressed the button to wake it up. Nothing happened. I'd forgotten my phone was dead.

"Damn!" I flung the phone to the ground.

"No need to call it in, son." The sheriff's drawl from behind me. "Turn around slow, with yer hands where I can see 'em."

CHAPTER TWELVE

James

Sheriff Wallace was not happy with me.

"We used to have a sleepy little town here." He took off his wide-brimmed hat and rubbed a hand over his sandy buzz cut. A dark tan jacket hung unzipped over a khaki shirt that was struggling to contain his substantial bulk.

We stood at the outer edge of the clearing, twenty feet or so from the body.

"Now we've got you," he drawled, "some kinda homicide magnet, bringin' murder and mayhem from the big city."

I gave a one-shoulder shrug—my other arm was occupied with hanging onto Ginger—and resisted rising to the bait. "Not my idea of fun either, Sheriff."

He harrumphed and stomped off to confer with the coroner.

It felt like I stood there a good hour, shivering slightly in my lightweight jacket, my fingers having long since gone numb where the bailing twine was wrapped around them. The sheriff meanwhile had conferred with just about everyone in sight, including several crime scene techs and some EMTs.

Finally he came back over to me. "Let's go to the house. No doubt Ms. Johnson, er, Peterson is worried sick."

As we walked silently toward the house, I tried to figure out why he thought Carrie would be worried? Did he know something, or was it only a figure of speech?

A young female deputy let us in. Carrie and Phillip had gotten their acts together. Their eyes were red-rimmed and they were a bit jumpy, what one would expect of people who'd received the news that a family member had been murdered. But their behavior didn't seem suspicious, to me at least.

I wasn't ready to breathe a sigh of relief just yet though. The sheriff was no dummy.

Hat tucked under his arm, he asked if they could search the house.

Something flickered in Carrie's eyes but otherwise she kept her cool and nodded.

I would have felt proud of her if I weren't still pissed that she'd lied to me, and terrified that she'd be arrested.

Wallace nodded to the female deputy and tilted his head to the right. She headed that way, toward the hallway and Phillip's room. The sheriff looked at Bill Harris and lifted his bushy eyebrows toward the ceiling. Bill, frowning, climbed the stairs to the second floor.

Sheriff Wallace gently questioned Carrie and the boy. They both denied leaving the house this morning.

As he seemed to be winding down, Bill came down the stairs, carrying a large plastic bag. He glanced at me, then quickly diverted his eyes.

My heart stuttered in my chest. *What has he found?*

Carrie looked relieved when Bill held up the bag. It contained a pair of pink slippers.

I glanced down at her feet. She was now wearing white socks and loafers.

A quick glance at Phillip's feet. The bottom of his jeans covered the upper part of hiking boots. I prayed no one would notice. It was strange footwear for inside.

The sheriff took the slippers from Harris and examined them through the bag. "Looks like some blood on these."

"Yes, Sheriff," Carrie said. "I dropped a glass on the floor in the bathroom this morning. Cut my foot on one of the broken pieces."

It sounded good. A fine piece of acting. But I knew her tell now. Her eyes were too wide, attempting to look innocent.

The sheriff lifted an eyebrow at her explanation. "Don't be makin' any travelin' plans for a little bit yet, Ms. Johnson. I mean, Mrs. Peterson." He turned to me. "You goin' anywhere any time soon?"

"I've got some auditions coming up, in DC." Now that the threat of Greg was gone, I wasn't about to put my career on hold indefinitely. "But I'll come back here afterwards."

Sheriff Wallace's gaze held mine for a beat, then he nodded. He gestured for Deputy Harris to lead the way to the front door.

Once there, the sheriff turned. "My condolences, ma'am." He tipped his head toward Phillip. "To you too, son."

Bill nodded to Carrie, still avoiding my eyes. They both donned their hats and went out, closing the door behind them.

Carrie sank down in a heap on the sofa and let out a big sigh.

"Shh." I pushed aside the curtain to watch the sheriff walk slowly to his cruiser.

Where was Bill Harris? Oh, there he was, hiking back toward the woods.

"We need to be really careful," I said, still looking out the window, "not to let on how relieved we are."

"Why shouldn't you two be relieved." Phillip's voice was hostile. "My dad's dead. Now you can go at it, no holds barred!"

I pivoted.

The boy was standing near his mother, rigid, his fists clenched at his sides.

"Phillip," I said, trying to keep my voice gentle, "we're not glad that your dad is dead, but we can't help being relieved that the threat to ourselves is gone." Perhaps that was more honesty than he could handle at this point, but I wasn't inclined to sugarcoat things.

Carrie shook her head slightly, her eyes shiny. "Talk about mixed emotions."

Phillip abruptly sat down beside her. Then, to my surprise, he nodded. In the next instant, he was sobbing in her arms.

I slipped as quietly as I could out of the room. The boy had a right to his grief.

⊷◇⊶

Carrie

I'm a terrible mother sometimes. Even before Phillip had calmed down some, all I could think about was the need to get out of the house. We'd been cooped up here for too long.

I did my best to comfort him. As his sobs subsided, I suggested that we go get some groceries. I had another reason for needing to get out of the house with some legitimate errand as cover.

"Let's go to Winchester," James said. "We still need to be on guard some, but we can relax a little more there. And they have a Giant."

His point was well taken. In Paxtonburg, we had limited choices, only a couple of independently owned grocery stores. And Winchester, a larger town about an hour away, suited my other purpose as well.

We still hadn't had breakfast, and the smell of burnt eggs emanating from the kitchen was off-putting.

"First, IHOP," James said, with false enthusiasm.

"Let me get my jacket and purse." I went up to my bedroom first and retrieved a black vinyl tote bag from my closet. I grabbed my wallet out of my purse and dumped it in the bag, then went back downstairs.

In the living room, James had his back to me, talking about his Mustang to Phillip, probably trying to keep the boy's mind off his grief for a while.

My heart warmed but I didn't linger. Phillip's eyes followed me as I headed toward the kitchen.

I grabbed a paper grocery bag from the floor of the pantry and snagged my jacket from the hook by the back door. I peeked out the doorway. I could see James, in profile, still talking. I caught the word *Mustang* again.

Phillip saw me as I started down the hallway. He quickly asked James a question.

I searched the study, now my son's improvised bedroom. I was getting a little frantic when I noticed something different about the long bookcase that stretched along one wall. The books on one of the shelves were not as I'd left them last time I'd dusted. They were usually pushed back, with some knick-knacks in front of them. Now their spines were lined up neatly along the outer edge of the shelf, and the knick-knacks were on the shelf above.

You clever boy!

I said a silent prayer of thanksgiving that the younger female deputy had searched his room, not the more experienced Bill Harris. She had been very neat. Few things were disturbed.

I pulled the books off the shelf. The sneakers, rolled-up sweat pants, and crumpled white tee-shirt were lined up along the back edge of the shelf.

Unfortunately, only the sneakers and tee-shirt fit in my tote bag and still allowed the snap at the top to close. I'd figured that would be the case, thus the grocery bag.

I refolded the sweat pants, getting them as flat as possible, and slid them into the paper bag. I held the bundle against my chest while buttoning my jacket over it. I suspected I looked like I'd gained twenty pounds. I slung the tote bag over my shoulder. It would pass for a purse.

Out in the living room, I moved to the door as quickly as I could. "Let's go. I'm starved."

At the car, I stood back, wrapping my arms around myself as if I were cold. "You take shotgun, Philly." I knew I wouldn't be able to hide the bundle from James if I sat up front, and I wanted him to have... what did they call it, *plausible deniability*?

Phillip as well, although he'd seemed to have figured out what I was doing.

Halfway to Winchester, I saw my chance when I spotted a McDonald's up ahead. "Hey, can you pull in there? I need a restroom."

James glanced in the rearview mirror. He raised an eyebrow at me. But then he said, "Sure," and made the turn.

I bolted from the backseat as soon as he'd stopped. Making sure to keep my back to the car, I hurried across the parking lot and into the building.

It was almost noon and the restaurant was busy. No one paid me a bit of attention.

In the ladies' room, one booth was occupied but no one was out by the sinks. I dumped the sneakers and tee shirt into the trash can, then pulled the grocery bag from under my jacket and shoved it down in. I grabbed a bunch of paper towels from the metal container on the wall and crumpled them on top.

Back in the Mustang, I blew out a slow sigh. Hopefully any incriminating blood on my son's clothes was now beyond the reach of the police.

I rested my head back against the headrest and used a relaxation technique I'd learned from one of those hundreds of self-help books I'd read, focusing on each group of muscles and willing them to relax.

It felt so good to let go of some of the tension.

It was past twelve-thirty by the time we got to the IHOP and had placed our orders.

With the enthusiasm unique to teenage boys, my son plowed into the stack of pancakes before the waitress's hand was completely withdrawn. She let out an indulgent chuckle and put laden plates down in front of James and me.

The omelet on my plate looked delicious and my stomach growled. It had been a long morning with no breakfast. Then I noticed the bacon was underdone, still pink in places.

Raw meat.

My mind flashed to Greg's bloody body and my stomach heaved.

I shoved the image aside and took a bite of toast, figuring some food in the hollow space might quell the nausea. Half a slice of toast later, I felt up to nibbling on small bites of egg and cheese.

"I thought you were so hungry," James said.

"I was. I am." I took a bigger bite and tried to give him a reassuring smile. It felt a little off kilter.

James smiled back, then his eyes cut to Phillip across the table and his face sobered.

I followed his gaze.

With more than two-thirds of the pancakes gone, Phillip's fork had stopped halfway to his mouth. He dropped it with a clatter and his face crumpled.

James nudged the pile of extra napkins the waitress had left in the boy's direction. Then he diligently applied himself to his food, giving Phillip some privacy to snuffle into the napkins.

I ducked my head and took another bite of egg, although it tasted more like soggy cardboard at this point.

Surely I would grieve eventually, probably more for the dreams I'd had as a young and foolish bride than for the actuality of my marriage. But right now I mainly felt relief. Despite my queasy stomach, I felt lighter than I had in years.

But my son had lost his father.

"Sorry," Phillip mumbled as he wiped his nose with one of the napkins.

"No need to apologize," James said softly. "Grief is like that. You kinda forget it's there, and then it slams into you from behind."

My heart swelled and I squeezed James's thigh under the table. His hand found mine and he squeezed back.

Phillip was looking at us now, his eyes red-rimmed and hollow with pain. "How long does it last?"

"I don't know," James said softly. "Mine isn't over yet."

He was referring to Annaleise. I suspected that was a loss deep enough it would always hurt some.

I put down my fork and reached across the table to touch my son's arm. "A long time, I'm afraid. I lost my father when I was only a little older than you. It hurts off and on for a long while. But the periods in between get longer, and then one day you think of him and it's just with fondness, not pain anymore. Then some good things happen in your life, and you realize you can be happy again."

I didn't tell him that the good thing that drove away the last of my grief for my father was Greg's whirlwind romance, and the false promises for happiness he'd showered on me.

By the end of the meal, James had gotten Phillip going on corny knock-knock jokes. We were all giggling when the waitress brought the check.

She gave us a big smile. "Y'all have a great day now."

At the car, Phillip got in the back seat. He was silent as we drove to the grocery store.

I swivelled around. "Are you okay?"

"Yeah," he mumbled without looking at me.

Grocery shopping was uneventful. We loaded up James's trunk and headed for home.

Again, Phillip was silent, staring out the side window.

I dozed off.

When I woke, the familiar scenery said we weren't far from home. I glanced over my shoulder.

Phillip was still silently staring at the countryside.

James looked up in the rearview mirror, then at me. He gave a slight shake of his head and reached over to squeeze my hand, lying in my lap.

That subtle input, a little head shake, should have triggered, if anything, a sense of relief—I wasn't alone in my parenting anymore. Instead, heat blossomed in my chest. Phillip was my son, not his.

I squelched that thought. After all, I had hoped that James would take a fatherly interest in my boy.

The angry heat spread. My eyes stung a little and my throat tightened. Greg had been a terrible husband, but he'd been a good father, except for that whole beating-the-crap-out-of-your-mother-while-you're-watching thing.

If he'd only been a mediocre husband, I probably would have been content. I had wanted a normal family so badly, one in which people were nice to each other and there were no secrets, no elephants in the living room.

Instead I'd traded my mother's verbal abuse for far worse at Greg's hands, and now my son was fatherless.

Self-doubt niggled at the edge of my brain. Was I a better judge of men now? Greg had also been nice to me, before we were married.

Was there an abusive streak in James that I was ignoring? He'd grabbed me the other morning in the driveway, when Phillip and I were trying to run away... to save James from all of this.

I knew he cared about me, but would he keep standing by a woman whose life was such a train wreck?

"Oh shit!" James's words yanked me out of my reverie.

He pointed to the entrance to our shared lane. A sheriff's department cruiser was parked on the road's shoulder a few feet beyond it.

My heart plummeted into my stomach. "Can't we keep on driving?"

"I suspect that's why he's there," James said grimly as he turned into the lane.

I swivelled around and watched out the back window. Sure enough a silhouette of a deputy picked up a radio mic and talked into it.

Sheriff Wallace met us in my front yard. He waited until we were all out of the car, examining each of us up and down before making a move. It dawned on me that he was looking for weapons.

"I thought I told y'all to stay put," he said, his hands clasping his belt below his pot belly.

"We went grocery shopping," James said, his tone slightly annoyed. "I didn't think going to the Giant in Winchester constituted leaving town."

"Harrumph." The sheriff stepped over to me and took my elbow, not roughly but not gently either. "I'm afraid we need to ask you some questions, Mrs. Peterson." Then he added in a firmer voice, "At my office."

He started leading me to his own cruiser, parked in James's driveway.

Heart pounding, I frantically looked back over my shoulder.

James gave me a fake smile. "We'll put the groceries away and come to town to pick you up after the sheriff's done with his questions." His tone was neutral, as if we were discussing what to have for dinner. "You probably ought to wait until

Sam is there though, before you answer anything. I'll call him."

The sheriff paused, turned us both back toward James. "That's a good idea, y'all comin' to town. I may have some questions for you as well. You see, we found the murder weapon. Brought out a search dog and he dug it up right quick."

My knees almost gave out on me. The sheriff tightened his grip, holding me up.

CHAPTER THIRTEEN

James

Carrie and Sam were already in an interview room when Phillip and I got to the sheriff's office. No one would tell us anything, other than to take a seat and the sheriff would be with us shortly, followed by a distracted gesture toward a hard bench in the hallway.

I'd tried to get Phillip to stay at the house, but he'd refused.

Now, as we settled on the bench, I muttered to him under my breath. "Don't say a word about finding him, or the knife."

I knew that's what Carrie would want, to keep her son out of it.

That's why she'd incriminated herself with that damned robe. If she'd only wiped the knife and then buried it. Or better still, left it by the body.

Of course, I didn't know how else we would've disposed of a bloody terrycloth robe. It was too big to shred and flush, as she'd done with her nightgown.

I'd called Mary on our way into town. After filling her in, I asked her to get the detective to track down anyone who might be considered an enemy of Gregory Peterson.

"That'll be a long list," Phillip muttered as he listened to my end of the conversation.

I couldn't quite figure this kid out. But then what did I expect, rationality from a teenager? And a teenager who'd just lost his father, no less.

Who'd murdered his father maybe?

Suddenly Bill Harris was standing in front of me. "Come with me, please, Mr. Fitzgerald. We have some questions for you."

The formality of his speech didn't bode well.

I stood and half turned to Phillip. "Remember you can't talk to the boy without his mother present." Technically I was speaking to Harris, but the reminder was aimed at Phillip.

Harris led me to an interview room. I had a moment of uncomfortable *deja vu* as I flashed to the interrogation after Annaleise's murder. The similarity to my current situation was reinforced when the deputy sat down across from me, some photos upside down in front of him, as he had that day six months ago.

And his brown eyes were as hard and cold as marbles, as they had been then. He flipped the top photo over.

I winced a little, even though I'd seen the scene in real life—Greg's bloody body.

He flipped another photo over, shoved it toward me.

I leaned forward, squinted, even though I could make out the objects lying on a gray tarpaulin just fine. "What's this stuff?" I asked, my tone perfunctory. Being an actor definitely paid off at times.

He pointed to the object with a black leather handle. "Huntin' knife."

It's long, nasty-looking blade had flecks of red on it.

"You tell *me* what this is." He pointed to the other object.

A wad of pink terrycloth showing stains that ranged from orange to rust. Playing dumb, I said, "What is it?"

"Maybe this will help." He flipped a third photo on top, as if he were dealing stud poker.

The terrycloth robe had been spread out on the tarp. The stains were smears down the center, but not a spatter pattern. It registered that Sam could use this in Carrie's favor at trial.

If she'd killed Greg, there would be more specks of blood all over the robe. But how could Sam argue that she didn't commit murder, just hid the weapon, without implicating Phillip, the only plausible motive for wanting to hide the bloody knife?

Dear God, I hope this mess doesn't make it to trial. But I had a bad feeling it would.

"Recognize it?" Harris asked.

"It looks kind of like a robe Carrie has."

"Suppose I told ya Ms. Peterson has acknowledged it's hers."

I opened my mouth, although I had no idea what I was going to say. Wait, I'd seen lawyers on TV dramas use that "suppose I told you" trick. I clamped my mouth shut again.

Harris leaned forward. "Did ya kill to protect Ms. Carrie? After all, you've killed before to protect her."

Heat exploded in my chest. I glared at him. "I killed before to protect myself. Carrie had nothing to do with it. She came running when she heard the shots."

Harris leaned back again, grinning, a glint in his eye.

"It was ruled self-defense," I pushed through gritted teeth.

"Of course." The deputy waved his hand nonchalantly in the air. "Crime techs found blood in the drain of the upstairs shower."

The somewhat abrupt change of subject was no doubt intended to throw me off. It only half succeeded. "Carrie told you she cut her foot this morning."

Harris shrugged. "We'll see what the lab says when they've finished analyzing it."

My heart constricted as I tried not to let my anxiety show. The odds were good the lab would find Greg's blood in that drain. In which case, Carrie was screwed.

"Where'd y'all go in Winchester?" Harris asked.

"IHOP and then the Giant."

"You stop anywhere else, goin' or comin'?"

I was ready for the question and hoped my acting was up to standard. "Nope."

I wasn't about to tell him about Carrie's restroom break, during which I'm pretty sure she ditched Phillip's clothes from this morning. If it came out later, I'd say I'd forgotten to mention such an inconsequential stop.

A crisp knock on the door and it was flung open. Sam barreled in, huffing a little from the effort. "Now Deputy, you wouldn't be interrogatin' my client without me present, now would ya?"

"Not interrogatin', Sam." Harris gave him a smile that didn't reach his eyes. "Just a friendly chat."

Sam crooked his finger at me and I stood.

"Nice chatting with you, Deputy," I said to Harris. Sam and I left the room.

"Where's the boy?" Sam asked in a low voice.

"I left him there." I pointed, but the bench was now empty.

We found Phillip standing by a vending machine. He had a can of cola in his hand.

And a female deputy was chatting him up.

I prayed he hadn't said anything about stopping at McDonald's on the way to Winchester.

Sam insisted we come home with him for supper. "Maisie always cooks for an army, and we need to discuss strategy."

"Where's my mom?" Phillip said, an edge of panic in his voice.

"She has to stay in jail tonight," Sam said in a soothing voice, as he ushered us out the door of the sheriff's department. "She'll be arraigned tomorrow morning, and the judge will set bail."

Feeling a bit numb, I followed Sam's car in the Mustang, Phillip riding shotgun.

"I'm gonna tell them I did it," the boy said, his voice desperate.

"Did you do it?" I kept my tone mild.

He jerked his head around to look at me. "Um, yeah, I killed him."

I sighed. "This is getting old, Phillip. You're covering for your mom and she's covering for you, and I don't believe either one of you did it."

He stared at me, his mouth hanging slightly open. "Why not?"

"Because of the note on your window."

"But I went out there because of the note and–"

"And your mom followed you because of the note, which is exactly what the killer wanted you two to do. You were lured out there so that one or both of you would be blamed for your father's death."

"So the note would clear us. We shouldn't have burned it."

"Maybe, but what's done is done. Personally I think we're better off leaving the note out of this. To others, it will look like motive. Your father lured you out of the house. Your mother followed, found him trying to take you away and killed him."

"Okay, I'm confused," the boy said. "Why does the note convince you that we're both innocent then?"

"Because neither you nor your mom is stupid. If either of you had gone out there intending to hurt your father, you would have taken the note with you. Or you would've destroyed it when you got back to the house."

Phillip was shaking his head. He opened his mouth.

I kept talking. "And neither of you has said anything *at all* about your father's behavior, what he did or said before you killed him. You act like he was already dead when you got there, which is exactly what I think happened."

Sam pulled into his driveway and I parked the Mustang at the curb, then turned to Phillip. "Look, let this play out for a while. You can always claim you did it later, even though I don't believe you did. But give me some time to investigate, see if I can find out who really killed your father."

"So don't mention the note," he said. "What do I tell them if they find out I went into the woods?"

I shrugged. "You got tired of being cooped up in the house so you took a walk. You knew your father wouldn't hurt you, and if he tried to take you away, you'd just slip away from him again, like you did in the first place."

Phillip nodded.

"What did you tell that female deputy?"

"Nothing. She asked how I was holding up. I told her I was okay."

"Good. Other than leaving out the note, and the night-gown in the toilet, tell Sam the truth."

I started to open my car door. Phillip grabbed for my arm. "James, what if they convict her?"

"I don't think that'll happen, son." I kept my voice steady, even though my own heart had gone into overdrive at the thought. "I'm going to do my damnedest to keep it from happening."

He swallowed hard, his barely-formed Adam's apple bobbing in his throat. Then he nodded and we got out of the car.

Inside the house, Sam ushered us into his study.

"Dinner in thirty minutes," Maisie called out, as her husband was closing the study door.

"Okay, run it all past me again," Sam said, as if we'd already told him our stories. He grabbed an unlit stogie from a crystal ashtray on the desk.

"What did Carrie say?" I asked before Phillip could respond.

Sam glared at me.

"Tell us what his mother said." My tone was emphatic.

Sam closed his eyes, shook his head. "Yer gonna be the death of me, boy. I'm an old man, ya know. I could have a heart attack any day now, if you listen to that quack of a doctor Maisie drags me to."

"Sam," I said, my voice now placating, "I'm not trying to stress you out. But don't you think we should *start* with what Carrie told the sheriff."

Sam sighed and waved to the two overstuffed armchairs to either side of the front of his desk.

Phillip and I sat down. I gratefully sank into the soft upholstery. It had been a long time since I'd sat on something more comfortable than a bench in an IHOP booth.

Sam sighed again as he settled into his padded desk chair. "She said she woke and went to the kitchen to start breakfast. She noticed that Ginger was gone and she went outside looking for her. She stumbled on her husband's dead body in the woods. She pulled out the knife, then panicked, wiped the handle clean and buried it, wrapped in her robe."

"My God," I blurted, "they believed that!"

"Hardly," Sam snorted, "but I wouldn't let her say anything else when they kept hammering her." He turned to Phillip. "So what really happened?"

The teen said his rehearsed lines fairly well, claiming he'd gotten claustrophobic and went for a walk. "I found..." his voice choked, "I found him and pulled out the knife. It was..." He dropped his head into his hands and sobbed.

I reached across the gap between us and squeezed his shoulder.

"It was in his stomach," he said, barely above a whisper. He lifted his head. "Then Mom showed up and she musta thought I'd killed him. She grabbed the knife and told me to go back to the house."

Sam turned to me. "And you were?"

"I was sleeping on the sofa. I woke up early and went over to my house to get more provisions. We were running low on food. I let Ginger out as I went. When I came out of my house, I called for her but she didn't come. I took the supplies back to Carrie's house. She was in the shower. I went back out to search for Ginger and found Greg in the woods."

It was the truth, just not the whole truth, and the events weren't quite in the right order.

I leaned forward, as best I could in the enveloping armchair. "Look, Carrie doesn't want Phillip involved. If we can keep him out of it..." I trailed off, not sure how we would do that.

Sam's expression was thoughtful. He transferred the cigar from one side of his mouth to the other.

It crossed my mind to worry that he might get lip or tongue cancer from chewing on the damn things.

After a full minute, he said, "If we leave out the part where Phillip went for a walk, we have no explanation for why Carrie wrapped the knife in her robe and buried it."

"Unless Carrie heard me calling for Ginger," I said, "and came out looking for the dog, found the body and thought I'd tangled with Greg and killed him."

Phillip's eyes went wide. "That's no good. They'll think you did it!"

I was pleased he objected so strenuously to that possibility. Maybe I was starting to grow on the kid.

"Sam," I said, my voice firm, "I've got a P.I. investigating. I think both Phillip and I should refuse to say anything more until we get some word back from him."

Sam looked at me, his mouth working on the cigar. "I hope that detective is quick."

"Dinner," Maisie called, her voice muffled by the closed door.

Sam stood. "By the way, going to Winchester was a bad idea. Joe Wallace don't like it when folks don't do what he says." He arched his eyebrows. "And now he's curious as to why y'all did that."

CHAPTER FOURTEEN

James

Phillip and I arrived at the arraignment early, hoping to get a glimpse of his mother before the proceedings began.

Sam met us in front of the courthouse and took the clean outfit I'd brought. Without a word, he headed up the steps and into the building.

Once we were through security, he pointed to big double doors. "Go have a seat," he said gruffly. "I gotta talk to my client."

I wondered what had him in such a foul mood.

Ten minutes later, a matron brought Carrie in, wearing the dress and shoes I'd brought.

She glanced our way before being led to the defense table. We gave each other fake smiles.

I patted Phillip's shoulder. He tensed under the contact.

Sam bustled in from the back of the courtroom. He pushed through the wooden gate that separated the actors in the play from the audience and sat down next to Carrie. They tilted their heads together and conferred for several seconds.

The judge entered—a different one than we'd seen the other day, this one a wiry man with salt and pepper hair. Everyone rose.

A bailiff muttered some things. They didn't register in my mind. My eyes were on Carrie. She was an average-sized woman, about five-seven, but somehow today she seemed smaller.

The charges were read, murder in the second degree. The judge asked for a plea.

"Not guilty, your Honor," Sam said.

"Recommendations for bail?" the judge asked.

My throat was so tight I couldn't swallow.

"The state asks that the defendant be held without bail," the prosecutor said. "She has minimal ties to the community and has fled from adversity in the past."

"Your Honor," Sam objected, "she fled from an abusive husband, not from the law. Her son is certainly a tie to this community and she has made friends." He gestured toward Phillip and me.

It sounded lame to my ears. My whole body clenched, waiting for the judge to say Carrie would have to spend the weeks until her trial in jail.

"She plans to make Paxtonburg her permanent home," Sam added.

"Plans to and has are two different things, Counselor," the judge said.

The prosecutor looked smug.

Sam said, "She's been a resident of this county for eight—"

A blonde woman jumped up from the second row. "Your Honor, I'm Toni Hamilton. I was Gregory Peterson's fiancée. I request temporary custody of his son, Phillip. His father would want me to take care of him."

I felt my mouth fall open.

The judge blinked, twice.

"Your Honor," Sam quickly said, "this is hardly the time or place for this. But nonetheless, I don't think a custody issue is relevant. As I said, Ms. Peterson has ties to the community and has no reason to flee."

Anger seethed in my chest and made my stomach roil. This Toni woman had helped Greg Peterson find us, and even with Peterson dead, she was trying to muck things up.

The prosecutor opened his mouth, but the Toni bitch cut him off.

"The boy's father is gone." She sniffed and waved a small designer handbag in the air. Her black leather jacket and short red dress looked expensive, but they were too tight around her curvy figure. "If his mother's in jail," she sniffed again, but it was lousy acting, "who will look out for him?"

"Your Honor," Carrie's voice screeched with panic, "I want James Fitzgerald to take care of my son in my absence."

"This woman is a murderer," Toni bitch yelled. "She can hardly dictate what is best for the boy."

The judge waved his gavel in the air, his mouth open, trying to get a word in.

Sam stood up far straighter than one would expect his roly-poly body to allow. "Your Honor," he said emphatically, "Ms. Peterson is only *accused* of murder. She has not yet been convicted and should in no way have her parental rights impaired. The court should respect those rights in this matter."

The judge slammed his gavel down. "This is *not* family court!" he bellowed. He gave Toni a hard look. "And the issue is moot, for now. Bail is set at $200,000."

I hid a smirk as relief washed through me. I suspected the judge had been leaning toward siding with the prosecution, but granting bail silenced the blonde bitch disrupting his courtroom.

My stepfather had been quite well-to-do, but he'd left most of his money to charity, probably to spite me. Two hundred thousand was almost all I had left in my trust fund, the fund I'd never touched except to cover the expenses of maintaining the Virginia house, which had been in my mother's family for three generations.

I caught Sam's eye and nodded. He spoke in Carrie's ear. She looked my way, her eyes wild.

I tried to give her an encouraging smile, but my heart was thudding. The woman I loved had just been formally charged with murder.

Carrie

Two hours after my arraignment, I stepped out of the sheriff's department's jail a semi-free woman.

I took a deep breath. No matter how well kept a jail may be, it smells—of sweat and fear, if nothing else.

I was amazed that I was free. I was even more amazed that I was accused of murder. How had my life come to this point?

I spotted Phillip and all other thoughts fled from my mind. I bolted down the steps and grabbed him up into a hug.

Then I felt other arms around both of us. It took a moment to register.

James.

Guilt twisted my gut. My God, he was my rescuer, the man who'd paid my bail. And yet he hadn't been my first thought. All I'd seen as I'd walked out of that jail was my son.

How could I say I loved the man when...

James turned me toward him and planted a kiss on my lips. Something melted inside my chest.

Okay, I loved him, but not as much as I loved my son. Maybe that was as it should be.

Before I could finish sorting out my feelings, Sam stepped up beside me and cleared his throat.

"I got some bad news just before court." The spring day was relatively cool, but he took out a handkerchief and wiped his brow. "Sheriff Wallace sent a deputy over to Winchester to follow in your footsteps. She found a waitress at IHOP who said you all were laughin' it up over your late breakfast."

My heart plummeted to my toes.

"We were only trying to distract the boy from his grief," James said, his tone defensive.

Sam scowled at him.

"It's true." Phillip's voice was a bit shrill. He ducked his head, his cheeks turning pink. "I was crying," he mumbled. "James started telling jokes to cheer me up."

"It's a shame the waitress didn't see the crying part," Sam said. "You willing to testify, boy, if need be?"

I opened my mouth to protest, but Phillip was already responding. "Sure, if it'll help."

"Ask the waitress if she found the wad of wet napkins when she cleared the table," James said angrily.

Sam held up a hand. "I believe ya, son. It's not a good development, but we can deal with it. I just hope there won't be no more surprises hidin' in the bushes."

I felt nauseous. If Sam only knew how many things we hadn't told him.

James's shoulders drooped as his anger deflated. He turned to me, a false smile plastered on his face. "Let's go."

All the way home I prayed that the deputy "following in our footsteps" didn't figure out that we'd stopped at McDonald's so I could use the ladies' room.

I made us lunch, and then I laid down to take a nap. Jail is not conducive to a good night's sleep.

When I woke, James was curled up beside me. I don't know if he'd been asleep or not, but when I stirred, he rolled over and propped himself up on one elbow, smiling down at me.

"How you feeling?" he said, his voice soft and deep.

I arched my back, stretching my arms up above my head until my knuckles hit the headboard. "Better."

His smile broadened. He leaned down and kissed me on the forehead.

My skin tingled where his lips had been, but a warning signal shot through my brain and set my heart racing. He was my rescuer, and men who rescue you tend to exact a price for their care.

I pushed myself up to a sitting position, arms wrapped around my knees. "James..." I knew we needed to talk, to set some boundaries, but I didn't know where to start.

He followed my lead and propped himself against the headboard with some pillows.

"Where's Phillip?" I asked suddenly a little panicked. We were both fully clothed, on top of the comforter, and James had left the door open. But still I didn't want to upset my son any further than the last few days' events had already.

"He took Ginger for a long walk," James replied. "Said he wanted to explore his new home."

Now that it was safe was left unsaid.

"Look, James, I really appreciate all your help and support. And of course I'm not going anywhere, so you'll get your bail money back–"

"I'm not worried about that."

"What I'm trying to say is that you don't have to keep involving yourself in my mess. I'll..." I'd do what? Hire my own lawyer. With what money?

The frisson of warning threatened to turn into a full-fledged panic attack. I edged a bit away from him, only half realizing I was doing so.

He put a hand on my shoulder.

I flinched.

He gently turned me a little toward him. "Carrie, what is going on?"

I shook my head, more from frustration than anything. "I'm not sure. I only know that I can't let a man rescue me again."

He sat up and turned to face me, crossing his legs under him. "I don't see it as rescuing you. I see it as being partners. If I were in trouble, you'd do anything you could to help, wouldn't you?"

"Of course." I heard the slight tremor in my voice and knew I was way too close to tears. I cleared my throat and straightened my shoulders. "It's just that I need to do things my way with this."

His jaw clenched. "Meaning sacrifice yourself to protect Phillip. Carrie, I don't think he did it. It had to be somebody else, and I'm going to find out who."

I tried to laugh but it came out sounding more like a cackling chicken. "There you go rescuing me again. I–" I stopped abruptly, trying to sort out my tangled emotions. "I can't stand feeling this indebted. It makes me too vulnerable. Like I have to put up with anything because I owe you."

He stared at me for a beat. "So if I started putting you down or beating on you," his voice was tense, hurt and angry, "you'd have to take it."

He threw his hands up in the air and I flinched away.

Letting out a small groan, he jumped up off the bed and paced back and forth beside it. "How long do we have to be together before you stop thinking I'm going to do that?"

I took a deep breath, gathering my thoughts. "It's not that I *think* it. Intellectually I know better, or at least I believe you are different. But my gut keeps telling me that I've believed that before, and I was wrong."

He turned and stared at me. "So you don't believe your own perceptions of me?"

I nodded. "It's not that I don't trust you. I don't trust myself to know who to trust."

He rubbed the back of his neck. "And how do I fight that?"

I deflated, my head hanging down, shoulders rounding. "I guess you can't really. I know I'm a mess."

He closed the gap to the bed in one stride. "No, you're not. You're a beautiful, loving woman who's been mistreated all your life."

I gave him a small smile. "Thank you for saying that."

"I'm not just saying it. It's true."

"Well, like I said, you don't have to keep helping me straighten out my messes."

He sat down on the edge of the bed and reached for my hand.

I let him take it, suppressing the urge to flinch, which was weaker now.

"Carrie, I don't think of it as just helping you. I'm helping *us* get this straightened out so we can be together." He dropped his gaze, stared at our clasped hands. "I realized something over the last few days. Actually I realized it that morning last week, when you tried to leave."

"I was trying to spare you all this trouble," I quickly said.

He held up his free hand in a stop gesture. "I know." He dropped the hand and used his index finger to trace the veins on the back of my hand. A warm shiver ran up my arm.

"What I realized... Remember I said I've loved three women in my lifetime?"

I nodded even though his eyes were still on our hands.

He threaded his fingers through mine. "The first was my mother. I guess that's every boy's first love. When it felt like she'd chosen my stepfather over me, I told myself I didn't need them. I had Annaleise and my other friends. My family of choice."

Wind chimes tinkled.

One corner of James's mouth quirked up but his eyes remained solemn. "I thought I could never love anyone the way I did her. We'd been best friends for two decades. She was like my arm or my leg. I would've taken a bullet for Annaleise." He paused, glanced sideways at me. "But at no time after she died did I feel like I couldn't go on without her. It felt hard at times, but not impossible."

He looked up, met my gaze. "But you, Carrie... *You*, I cannot live without."

Warmth spread through me as his eyes held mine—and a sense of peace I'd never known before.

He let go of my hand and bracketed my cheeks with his palms, pulling me toward him. His kiss was gentle but deep, pulling me under. My body felt like it was melting.

His lips never leaving mine, he leaned me back and stretched his lean body beside me.

I rolled over and wrapped my arms around his neck. I never wanted the kiss, the moment, to end.

A cough from the hallway. "Mom, what's for dinner?"

I rolled away from James, gasping for air and pulling at my disheveled clothing.

James chuckled.

I smacked his shoulder and wiggled off the bed.

Phillip wasn't in sight. He'd apparently stopped short of the doorway when he'd realized I wasn't alone.

"I, um, haven't decided yet," I said. "What would you like?"

A beat of silence. "Meatloaf?"

"Sure, there's time to make one. I'll start on it now."

"Okay," Phillip called from the hall, still staying away from the open doorway. "I'll be in my room."

I looked down at James. His eyes were dancing, his cheeks puffed and red from the effort not to laugh.

I smacked him playfully again, and he grabbed me and hauled me down on the bed.

We rolled around for a minute or two, until I was able to extricate myself and head for the kitchen to start prepping dinner.

James

While Carrie cooked and Phillip once again retreated to his room to play video games, I sat in the living room and attempted to commune with a ghost.

"Annaleise?" I whispered.

A soft tinkling noise, as if she were whispering as well.

"Did you see who killed Greg Peterson?"

Silence for a beat. Then the wind chimes clanged dully, an almost mournful sound.

So ghosts are not omniscient, I thought. "You can only sense what's going on near where you are?" I whispered.

The wind chimes tinkled, sounding more normal.

Again, my use of *normal* and *ghost* in close juxtaposition boggled my mind.

"And you mostly hang around me, but sometimes you stay near Carrie?"

More tinkling.

"Can you do me a favor?" I asked. "If Carrie and I aren't together, can you stick with her? Because I couldn't bear to lose her."

The wind chimes again, a bit louder, and a warmth surrounded me.

I relaxed into Annaleise's ghostly hug.

"Food's ready," coming from the kitchen, broke the spell.

I shivered as the warmth evaporated.

It had been a long and intense day, and despite her nap, Carrie was drooping over her plate at the table.

"Why don't you go on to bed?" I suggested. "Maybe read for a while."

With a wan smile, she took me up on the suggestion.

Phillip and I were finishing up the dishes, when the boy gave me a hard look, a silent message of some kind.

"What?" I said.

He glanced up at the rafters. "Not in here. Everything echoes."

He led the way into the cavernous living room and kept going to the front door.

I grabbed my jacket off the end of the sofa and followed him out onto the porch.

When he turned toward me, there was worry in his eyes.

I prepared myself to reassure him that his mother would be fine, that she wouldn't be convicted of murder, even though I wasn't totally convinced of that myself.

"You can't let that woman get custody of me."

"Wha'? Who? That Toni woman?"

"Yeah. She creeps me out." Despite the sweatshirt he wore, he held his arms close to his body, hands shoved into his pockets—as if he were cold, though the spring evening was mild.

"How so?" I asked, striving to keep my tone neutral.

"Um," the boy's gaze dropped to the porch floor. He scuffed the toe of a sneaker across a floorboard. "She, um, kinda came on to me."

"When?" I asked.

"A couple months ago, shortly before I left. It was one of the reasons I got out of there."

"Did she do anything? Did she touch you?" My voice was probably more strident than it should've been.

"No, nothin' like that. Just talk, but she can be pretty crude." He ducked his head. "I mean, she's hot, I guess. She teaches aerobics at night and goes to the gym a lot, so she's in really good shape."

My stomach heaved. If the woman had been nearby, I would've strangled her.

"Phillip," I said in a gentle voice, "I know books and movies make it seem cool for a young guy to..." I hesitated, not wanting to be too crude myself. "To attract the attention of an older woman. But it's not cool. It's just creepy, and a little scary. How old is this Toni?" I vaguely remembered from the P.I.'s report that she was in her thirties.

"About Mom's age."

"Okay, so if a man in his thirties propositioned a four-teen-year-old girl, what would we call it?"

"I'm almost fifteen."

"Okay, so a fifteen-year-old girl. Would we think that was cool?"

He grimaced. "God, no!"

"It's called child abuse, and it's no different when the genders are reversed."

He swallowed hard, nodded, his gaze down.

I put my hand on his shoulder, waited until he met my eyes. "I will do everything in my power to keep that woman away from you. But if it comes down to it, you may need to tell the authorities what she said to you."

He nodded again. "I can do that, if I have to." But his face was grim.

I hoped he wouldn't have to.

CHAPTER FIFTEEN

James

Phillip turned and took a step toward the door. "Oh, and by the way," he said, his back to me, "you and Mom, it's okay with me."

I slapped him gently on the shoulder. "Glad to have your approval."

He looked back at me. "Not sure I'd go that far, but I want Mom to be happy."

I grinned at him. "I'll take that for now."

My pants pocket buzzed. I pulled out my phone. *Mary*, the screen read.

"I gotta take this."

I waited until he had gone back inside before answering. "Hey, Mare. How you doing?"

"I'm okay. How are you guys holding up?"

"Not bad, all things considered. Any word from the P.I.?" I asked the question, even though I had little hope that he'd come up with something this soon.

"Yeah, as a matter of fact," Mary said. "He's fast, but I'm afraid that means he's also expensive."

I stifled a sigh. Women worrying about my finances was getting old.

"The business partner, Torenson—apparently they don't get along very well, according to their employees."

"Yeah, Carrie said they tended to bicker over how to run the business."

"Hmm, this sounded like more than bickering. A couple of long-term employees said that the bosses had escalated to screaming at each other the last few months, usually behind closed doors, although that only muffled the content of their words, not the volume all that much. Apparently they both have short fuses, but something shifted a little before Christmas."

"Hmm, that was before Phillip ran away," I said. "But that woman Toni was on the scene by then, I think."

"Yeah, the P.I. found out more about her too. The employees said she came to the warehouse occasionally, looking for Peterson, but she liked to flirt. And get this, there's no record of her existence before last summer."

"Oh really." Yet another woman who had reinvented herself. Was she running from an abuser like Carrie had been, or from the law?

Since she'd been attracted to Greg Peterson, I suspected the former. It was a common enough phenomenon, so much so that it was a trope in many plays—the woman continuously attracted to the bad boys, even though they abused and misused her.

Mary's voice brought me back to the conversation. "There's more. The partner's been out of town for several days. Nobody seems to know where he is."

"Hmm," I said. An awful lot of people were missing in action from Connecticut.

"The detective got ahold of a photo of Torenson, and of the Toni woman. I'll text them to you."

"I already know what Toni looks like."

"Bottle blonde, too much makeup?" Mary said, her tone slightly derisive.

"Nice figure but she wears her clothes too tight. She showed up at Carrie's arraignment this morning and tried to get temporary custody of Phillip while Carrie was in jail."

"Say what?"

"She didn't get very far since Carrie immediately said she wanted me to take care of the boy, and it all became a moot issue when the judge granted bail. Hey, tell the P.I. to dig as deep as he can on her, and the business partner."

"Will do. Is there anything else I can do to help?"

"No, we're fine."

"Can I come down this weekend and maybe cook up some meals for you to freeze?"

I opened my mouth to say don't bother, then caught myself. I'd just gotten pissed at Carrie for trying to turn down my help.

And I suspected Mary was lonely. Our group of friends had pretty much fallen apart after Annaleise and her husband were killed. Mary and I kept in touch and I ran into Todd, another actor, through work sometimes. We had lunch occasionally and I'd had dinner with him and his partner, Fred a couple of times when I was in DC overnight. But the other couple in the group no one had heard from in months.

We hadn't realized how much Annaleise was our glue until she was gone.

Wind chimes tinkled near my ear.

"What was that?" Mary said.

"Nothing. I was considering logistics. Yeah, this weekend should work, and it would be good to have some meals on hand if this all goes to trial." I was a lousy cook and I wasn't going to expect Carrie to feed me after a long stressful day as a defendant in a murder trial.

"Bring extra ingredients though. We've got a teenage boy to feed too."

Mary chuckled. "Duly noted. See you then. I'll call if I have more news from the P.I."

We signed off and I checked my watch. It was eight-thirty, borderline too late to call most people, but I knew Sam was still up.

I was starting to shiver slightly, my light jacket inadequate as the night deepened. But I didn't want Carrie overhearing me. I called Sam's cell instead of the house line, in case Maisie had gone to bed early.

"Hey, it's James. Sorry to call so late."

"No problem, son. What can I do for ya?" he drawled.

I heard air being blown out and wondered if he'd actually lit one of his stogies when Maisie wasn't looking.

"Can you write up something making it legally official that I'm Phillip's guardian in the event that Carrie can't take care of him?"

"Yeah, but do ya really think that's necessary just yet?" I'd noticed that his northwestern Virginia twang became more obvious in the evenings. No doubt, it had something to do with his after-dinner brandy, the one vice Maisie still allowed him.

"I do. I don't trust that Toni woman and Phillip asked me specifically this evening to not let him end up living with her." I wasn't going to share why. That was Phillip's story to tell, if the need arose.

"Okay, I'll get my paralegal to draw somethin' up tomorrow."

"Thanks, Uncle Sammy." I intentionally used my childhood honorary nickname for him.

A low throaty chuckle. "You're welcome, son. And by the way, we'll need to hire a criminal lawyer if this ends up in court. I don't have that background."

I read between the lines. Sam had refused to take any money for his services. "We're family," he'd said. But a criminal lawyer would cost big bucks.

"I know. I can afford it," I lied. "And I appreciate all you're doing for us."

Things were looking up, for my career at least. I'd called Charlie on Wednesday morning to say I was available again. He'd arranged an audition for Thursday, and it had gone well.

It wasn't an ideal part for me, but I could get into it. And I needed the money. Rehearsals started in two weeks.

I drove into town before going home, to buy steaks and wine to celebrate. I'd break out the grill when I got home, so Carrie could take the evening off from cooking.

As I was coming out of the liquor store, I almost ran head on into a man I'd never seen before. And yet he seemed familiar. Dark buzz-cut hair came down to almost a point at the middle of his hairline. His dark eyes, in a jowly, tanned face, were hard.

Otherwise there was nothing remarkable about him. Medium height, medium build.

"Excuse me," I said.

He mumbled something and stepped around me. I shrugged and headed for the small grocery store for the meat and some baking potatoes and salad fixings.

I was standing over the steaks, my hand reaching out to pick a package up, when it hit me. I got out my phone and brought up Mary's message.

Yup. Same jowly face and dark widow's peak. The man I'd almost mowed down was Greg Peterson's business partner, Allen Torenson.

What the hell was he doing in Virginia?

Before going home, I made an unscheduled stop at the sheriff's department.

Deputy Harris was headed out as I pushed through the door. He stopped dead in front of me and groaned. "What do you want?"

I stifled my anger and acted like everything was fine between us. "I need some information, Bill."

"I can't talk to you about an ongoing investigation, especially when your girlfriend's been charged for the crime."

"The prosecutor has to cough up all he has to the defense attorney anyway, doesn't he? What difference does it make if we find things out then or now?"

Harris shook his head, but he turned and led the way to an interview room.

Once we were settled across from each other at the table, I said, "Has the autopsy been done yet?"

He nodded.

"Anything interesting?"

A half shrug, but something flitted across his face.

"Come on, Bill, how in the hell did a hundred-twenty-pound woman knife a big man like Peterson?"

"Because he wasn't expecting her to," Harris said.

I narrowed my eyes at him. "How do you know that?"

Another half shrug. "Just a theory, to explain how it happened. He's a big macho guy, assumes he can overpower her. Isn't really expecting her to fight back."

"And did you find any defensive wounds on her, or any of his skin under her nails?"

He sat perfectly still for a moment. "You've been watchin' too much TV, Fitzgerald."

"Did you?" I insisted.

He shook his head.

"So he wasn't trying to overpower her and she knifed him?"

Yet another shrug, both shoulders this time. "No. We think she thought it all out, decided the best way to get rid of him once and for all was to lure him to meet her, act like she wanted to come home, and then when his guard was down, she sticks him in the gut with his own knife."

I resisted the urge to roll my eyes. I could no more imagine Carrie doing that than I could see her flying to the moon.

"Would a woman even have enough strength in her arm to penetrate his coat?" I said. "Especially if she couldn't do much in the way of a back swing that would telegraph what was about to happen. She'd have to thrust straight out from her body to take him by surprise. And there were multiple wounds. Again, that would take a fair amount of strength."

Harris held up two fingers. "One, there's adrenaline that would give her more than normal strength, and two, one of the blows—the M.E. suspects it was the first one—it wasn't through the coat. It was in the middle of his stomach, where the coat was hanging open. The other thrusts were through the coat, but they were probably after he was down. They had more force behind them, the M.E. said. And were at an angle that indicated she probably knelt beside him and..."

He wrapped both hands around an imaginary knife handle and mimicked plunging it downward.

I was still skeptical, but I dropped that topic. "Where was he carrying the knife?" I asked. "And how'd she get it away from him?"

"Don't know. We didn't find any sheath for it."

"So he was what, carrying it loose in his pocket? A super sharp hunting knife." My tone was snide. "Would've torn the shit out of the pocket and probably stuck him in the leg. Or did he have it down in his boot? Did you find any cuts on his ankle?"

"We figured she carried the sheath off somewhere."

"So she takes the knife with her, wraps it in her robe and buries it someplace a dog can sniff it out in no time," my voice was going up in pitch and volume but I couldn't seem to stop myself, "but she carries off the sheath and hides it so well you all still haven't found it?"

"Criminals do stupid things all the time," he shot back, "especially in the heat of the moment."

"What heat of the moment? I thought the theory was that she'd carefully planned this out. Don't you think she would've thought through the whole getting-blood-on-herself thing better?"

Bill Harris stared at me blank-faced. Too blank-faced. "She also could have stolen the knife," he pointed out in a long-suffering tone, "when she left him months ago, and she took it with her out to the woods that morning."

I took a deep breath. "How do you know it's Peterson's knife?"

"The kid recognized it." Harris pushed his chair back and stood. "Look, man, I'm sorry this is goin' down this way

for you. But we've got enough evidence to convict her."
Something flickered in his eyes. He broke eye contact.

My insides clenched. "What aren't you telling me, Bill?"

"There is a possibility she could get off. Well, she'd be facing an obstruction charge."

"Wha'? What are you talking about?"

"I found the boy's clothes that she tried to hide in that Mc Donald's bathroom. The lab has them now. The theory that the knife was stolen could apply to the kid too. I'd want a weapon if I was gonna trek all over the countryside lookin' for my missin' mom."

My first thought was how could he have found the clothes. I knew none of us had said anything about that unscheduled stop. Had the sheriff posted a deputy to watch us, who'd tailed us when we left?

"Of course," Bill was saying, "seeing her kid go to jail for murderin' his dad might not be her preferred outcome."

I opened my mouth, about to point out that her hiding the clothes proved her innocence, since she obviously feared the boy had done it. I caught myself and clamped my mouth shut again. Harris was right. That was definitely not Carrie's preferred outcome.

He turned and walked to the door, then stopped. His back to me, his hand on the knob, he said, "Peterson didn't have any defensive wounds either, and no skin or anything under his nails. He was taken completely by surprise."

He pulled the door open and left the room.

I contemplated the implications of what I'd learned as I walked, stomach churning, back to my car. Once there, I called Mary before heading for home. We exchanged greetings and I asked, "Anything new from the P.I. on the business partner?"

"No, he hasn't been able to locate him. Torenson called his secretary Monday morning and told her he'd had to go out of town over the weekend and he was still tied up. She was to clear his schedule for the week."

"I've found him, I think. I saw him here, in Paxton-burg." And, if he'd been "out of town" since the weekend, he could've been here when Greg was killed sometime Monday morning.

Phillip had said his father's skin was cool to the touch. I wondered what the M.E. had reported regarding time of death. I hadn't thought to ask Harris about that.

But he had to have been dead for a while, probably since the middle of the night. Yet more evidence in my book that neither Phillip nor Carrie killed him. They couldn't have gotten out of the house at that time without triggering the alarm, which would have woken me up. Their window of opportunity to do their foolish gallivanting in the woods had been while I was next door raiding my pantry. But I was the only one who could testify to that, and my word, as Carrie's boyfriend, probably wouldn't carry much weight.

"What's he doing there?" Mary asked, bringing me back to the moment. It took me a second to realize she meant Torenson.

"Good question. Ask the P.I. to check into other enemies Peterson may have had. I got the impression from Phillip that he had quite a few. I'll see if I can find out what Torenson is up to down here."

"Okay... James, be careful."

I smiled at the phone. "I always am, Mare. Talk to you soon."

By the time I pulled into our shared lane, I was no longer in the mood for a celebration, and it was almost six. Carrie had probably already started dinner.

I pulled into my driveway and took the groceries inside. Stashing the steaks in the freezer, I hoped we'd be in the mood to celebrate something soon.

I walked next door to Carrie's house, rang the bell, then let myself in with my key. I supposed ringing the bell was no longer necessary, but it had become a habit. And it seemed the polite thing to do.

As I entered the kitchen, Carrie was on her phone. "Sure, that will be fine," she said and disconnected.

"Who was that?" I asked.

"Allen Torenson, Greg's partner."

"What?" My voice screeched.

Carrie looked at me funny. "He wants to come out later this evening to discuss how to deal with the business."

I stood in the kitchen doorway, dumbfounded. Could the explanation for Torenson's presence in town be that simple?

CHAPTER SIXTEEN

Carrie

Phillip devoured yet another of his favorites, ham with mac and cheese. I nudged his salad bowl over in front of him.

He grimaced but then dove into it with almost as much gusto.

Meanwhile I seemed to have lost my appetite. Allen Torenson's phone call had brought home to me the enormity of everything I needed to deal with, above and beyond the court case. The business, Phillip's schooling, the house in Connecticut—which I would probably sell. Way too many bad memories there. And lurking behind all of those things was the question of where we would live. Would Phillip want to go home to his friends and his school?

If he did, then as a good mother I should do that. The kid had already had enough upheaval and heartache to last a lifetime.

But how could I leave James?

Would he be willing to move with us? We were as close to New York as this area was to DC. He could certainly find work there, but he wouldn't be as well known to the directors there.

Did I even have the right to ask him to uproot his life? Maybe we could try a long-distance relationship. He could come up when he was between plays, and I could come to Virginia when Phillip was with...

My chest tightened. Phillip wouldn't be visiting his father. I swallowed a small lump in my throat.

James was also picking at his food. At one point, he shifted in his chair and I noticed a bulky angular bulge in his right pants pocket.

With a jolt I recognized the outline of my gun. Well, his gun really, registered in his name, but he'd bought it for me.

Probably a good thing it was in his name or the sheriff would have confiscated it. I doubted a suspected murderer, out on bail, was supposed to have a firearm.

"Phillip," James spoke for the first time since we'd sat down, "you implied the other day that your father had enemies. Who did you mean?"

Phillip's hand stopped, his fork—stabbed through a cherry tomato—halfway to his mouth. He shrugged. "Nobody specific, but Dad was always getting into it with somebody. Even the clerks at the hardware store used to scatter when they saw him coming."

James looked at me. I shook my head. "Trust me, I've been wracking my brain. Lots of people had beefs with Greg. He wasn't an easy man to deal with. But I can't think of anyone who would have sufficient motive to kill him, especially if they had to track him down here."

Phillip had finished his salad. I stood and started gathering plates, my own only half empty. James lifted his to the top of the stack in my hands. It also had a good bit of food still on it. I put the plates in the sink.

Phillip had jumped up and was putting away leftovers.

I laid a hand gently on James's shoulder. "You okay?" I said quietly.

He nodded and patted my hand.

I tried again. "You seem preoccupied."

Phillip turned from in front of the fridge. "Everything's put away. You want me to do the dishes?"

"No, I'll get them later," I said.

Phillip nodded and took off for his room.

I walked to my chair opposite James's and sat down.

"Isn't Torenson going to be here soon?" he asked.

I glanced up at the kitchen clock. "In half an hour. What's going on?"

He shook his head slightly.

Suddenly anger bubbled in my chest, like hot lava, so intense it scared me. "Talk to me, James," I said through clenched teeth.

He startled a little, then tilted his head. And I realized I was overreacting.

"I'm sorry. It's just that Greg would never talk about anything, even in the early days before..." Before we were married and he started hitting me.

"I was trying not to worry you," James said.

"I'm a big girl, and I'm already worried as hell, so it can't get a whole lot worse."

His expression said he wasn't sure about that, but he said, "I learned some things from Bill Harris today."

"Oh?"

"What did you do with the sheath the knife was in?"

"What sheath?"

He raised an eyebrow. "You didn't bury it somewhere, did you?"

"I didn't even see any sheath." My voice was sharper than I'd intended.

"There wasn't one at the crime scene, and the dogs didn't find one in the woods."

I was still irritated, but now also curious. "So?"

"It's kinda odd, that's all. It looked like a sharp knife. Greg wouldn't have been carrying it around loose. It would have been in a sheath, most likely on his belt or in his boot. Was he wearing boots? I can't remember."

I closed my eyes for a second, envisioned the bloody scene in the woods. Then wished I hadn't when ham-flavored bile rose in the back of my throat. Swallowing hard, I said, "Yes, his hunting boots. And when he went hunting, he usually had one of his knives, *in a sheath*, on his belt."

James nodded, put his hands flat on the table and began to push himself to a stand. The expression on his face had my stomach churning.

"That isn't all, is it?"

Something flickered in his eyes. He sank back into his chair. "No. He had no defensive wounds, and nothing under his fingernails that would indicate he tried to fight anyone off."

He watched my face as I thought about that. I said, "So he didn't feel threatened by whoever it was. He let them approach."

"And get close enough to jam a knife into his gut."

I winced.

"Sorry," James said. "It had to be someone he knew and trusted. That's part of why the sheriff thinks it's you. He wouldn't have seen you as a threat."

Anger roiled in my stomach again, along with something else that it took me a moment to name. Shame.

It was true. I had been such a wimp with Greg that he wouldn't have felt any need to be on guard with me.

But I could think of other people he would let get that close. My heart stuttered in my chest. Our son was one of them.

James said, "How well do you know this Torenson?"

I shrugged. "Not extremely well. He's divorced. We didn't really socialize with him. Like I said, he and Greg fought about how the company should be run."

"Did they hate each other?" James asked.

"Oh no. They just squabbled a lot. It was more like siblings fighting."

Something flickered again in James's eyes. *Is he keeping something else from me?*

The doorbell rang.

Ginger had been sleeping on her bed in one corner of the kitchen. Now she jumped up and went ballistic. I grabbed her collar.

"I'll get it," James yelled over the barking. His face grim, he surreptitiously patted his pants pocket as he stood up.

Shushing Ginger, I said, "Why the gun?"

As he left the kitchen, James looked back over his shoulder. "The P.I. found out that the squabbling had escalated to screaming in recent months."

My stomach knotted as my brain digested the implications. Torenson a killer? I found it hard to believe. But the man did have a temper, although not as bad as Greg's.

Yet, there had been no signs of a fight. Allen grabbing Greg's knife during a struggle and sticking him with it—yeah, that I could imagine. But walking up to him and knifing him in cold blood. I found that hard to believe.

I felt nauseous. If I couldn't believe that of Allen Torenson, how could I have imagined for even a second that my son might do it?

I shuddered and belatedly called after James, "Bring him back here." Sitting on the living room sofa in a row, like the three see/hear/speak-no-evil monkeys, would not be conducive to a business discussion.

I told Ginger to lie down. She did so by the door, and I set about making coffee.

Allen Torenson was pretty much as I remembered him, medium build with dark hair. I couldn't recall his eye color, and I couldn't see his eyes as he came into the kitchen, his gaze down, with James close behind.

Then it hit me. *He's checking out my ass!*

Maybe I should've been flattered, but it pissed me off.

I seemed to be getting pissed off at everything lately, but then again I was under a lot of stress. It's not every week one gets arrested for murder.

When Allen finally looked up, his eyes were dark. And strange, almost lifeless.

We settled around the table with coffee mugs in front of us.

"I know you all have a lot on your plates," Allen said, "so I'll come right to the point and then I'll get out of your hair." Ironically, he paused and ran his hand over his own short hair.

The words sounded natural enough, informal, but his body was rigid.

"I've been trying to buy Greg out for some time," he continued. "He seemed to be losing interest in the day-to-day operations of the business."

That struck me as odd. Greg had loved his business, far more than he'd loved me. Only Phillip had seemed more important to him than the success of PT Construction. But he'd loved the company mostly for how it made him look good. It was possible he was getting bored with the actual running of it.

"I'd offered him three million for his half of the company, but I'm prepared to add another five hundred thousand to that." Allen waved his hand in a vague gesture. "Not so much because it's worth that much, but since Greg has died... Well, to help pay for the boy's education."

I was about to ask if the company had been appraised recently, but James spoke up first. "The *boy* is Greg's heir, is he not?"

Shame heated my face. I wasn't sure why, and that triggered more anger in my gut. "I'm Phillip's guardian." *Guardian?* Why'd I pick that word? Technically correct but... I'd been hanging around lawyers too much lately.

James shot a glance in my direction, something in his eyes I couldn't quite decipher. "He should probably be in on this conversation." His tone was mild.

The anger spluttered in my chest, searching for a target. Finding none, I set my lips in a grim line and nodded.

James left the kitchen.

Allen and I sat in an uncomfortable silence. I stared at my coffee cup. This was not going as I'd imagined.

When I snuck a peek at Allen, I caught him eyeing my breasts.

Thank God, James returned at that moment, my son in tow.

"Phillip, do you remember Mr. Torenson?" I said.

"Yes. Hello, sir." His expression was guarded.

Allen nodded without saying anything.

James and Phillip took their seats at the table.

"Can I have some coffee, Mom?"

"It'll keep you up."

"No more than us," James said, again in that damned mild tone.

I glared at him. But I got up and fetched another mug, filled it from the pot and put it in front of my son. He reached for the cream pitcher.

Of course Phillip wanted the caffeine for the same reason we did, to keep him alert during an important business meeting.

A cacophony of emotions erupted inside of me. My chest swelled with pride, even as my throat tightened and my stomach twisted. My son was being forced to grow up too soon.

Then again, watching one's mother being beaten on a regular basis was hardly conducive to childhood innocence.

"As I was telling your mother," Allen Torenson said, "I offered your father three million dollars for his interest in the company, and I'm willing to sweeten that with another five hundred thousand."

Phillip's eyebrows went up and he looked at me. "How much is the company worth, Mom?"

"I don't know." I turned to Allen. "Has there been a recent appraisal of its assets?"

"Uh." His gaze shifted away from mine. "We had it appraised a little while ago. That's what the three million for half was based on."

"How long ago?" James's voice now had a sharp edge.

"A few months."

"How *many* months?" James said.

"Um," Torenson glanced from James to me, "I'd have to look it up."

James frowned. "Mr. Torenson, as you said, we've got a lot on our plates right now." He started to push up from the table. "We'll think about it and get back to you."

Heat rose from my chest and into my face. I tamped it down and held out my hand in a stop gesture. "Phillip, do you have any desire to follow in your father's footsteps?"

James cocked his head at me, then sank back into his chair.

"Uh, I don't know," Phillip said. "He wanted me to."

"Do you have any questions about how the company is run or what Mr. Torenson and your father did each day to keep it going?"

"Um, not right now."

I nodded and gave him a smile.

James leaned back in his chair. "Mr. Torenson..."

I expected him to try again to bring the discussion to a close. I was ready to let him do so now.

But that wasn't where he was going. "Your partner had enemies." His tone was almost casual. "Who were they?"

Allen's eyes went wide. He stared at James. After a beat, he said, "Not enemies exactly. But sometimes he was a hard person to like."

"Anyone who would want him dead?" James asked.

Allen's body stiffened. "No."

An awkward silence stretched out.

Finally, I said, "Allen, my son and I will need to talk some more about the business, so it may be a bit before we can give you an answer. It occurs to me that if Phillip wants to go into construction, it would be a lot easier to do so if he already owned half interest in a construction company."

Allen's lips pursed and his eyes narrowed. Then his face went blank—too blank. "Three and a half million is a generous offer."

James opened his mouth, but I cut him off. "I'm sure it is. We'll get back to you as soon as we can."

Allen stood. James and I both rose.

Allen turned to James, as if dismissing me. "My offer won't stay on the table forever." His words were clipped.

Anxiety rippled through my body. That tone, coming from Greg, even if aimed at someone other than me, had meant I would be beaten within the next twenty-four hours.

I gritted my teeth and mentally shook off the irrational fear. Under it, anger seethed at Allen's dismissal. "Has the company gone down or up in value, since it was appraised?" My own tone was terse.

It might have been my imagination but Allen seemed to pale a little under his permanent tan. "It's stayed about the same."

We'll see about that. There would definitely be a new appraisal. But for now I nodded, one crisp up and down of my head, and turned to lead the way out of the kitchen.

James followed us across the living room.

Phillip stayed behind. Cups clattered in the sink. My throat tightened for a moment as an insight hit me. He was so good at cleaning up dishes because he hadn't wanted Greg to have a dirty kitchen as an excuse to beat me.

Allen Torenson said nothing at the door, just gave us a sharp nod and left.

As soon as the front door closed behind him, James said, "What an ass."

I turned to him. He was standing close behind me. Too close.

Adrenaline shot through me. I sucked in air, made an effort to steady my voice. Why was I so jumpy tonight?

"I'd forgotten that Allen's a bit of an odd duck." He always seemed rather stiff, his words scripted, as if he were from a different species and didn't quite know how to interact with humans.

"An odd, creepy, asshole of a duck," James said with a smile.

A sharp bark of laughter came out of my mouth, and I felt myself beginning to relax.

"I'm proud of you."

My mouth drop open. That was probably the last thing I'd expected him to say. "For what?"

"For standing up to him." James took my hand. His eyes went soft, and he lowered his lips to mine.

I wanted to pull back, but my body had other ideas. It leaned into him. James was an affectionate man, something I'd never known before. Even my father, who'd loved me dearly, had done so in a brusque, non-demonstrative way. But James normally touched me often—a hug, a kiss, a pat on the hand, no matter what we were doing at the time.

Phillip's presence had constrained that lately. I'd missed the touching.

The kiss deepened and James wrapped his arms around me. My insides turned to liquid, but in a good way. Lust, not fear this time. Muscles relaxed some more, letting me know just how tense they had been. Heat enveloped me.

A small part of my brain was clamoring for attention. *You're mad at him, remember?*

But I couldn't, at the moment, recall why.

He broke the kiss and led me to the sofa. We settled there, his arm around my shoulders. I rested a hand on his thigh.

It tensed and jiggled slightly under my touch. A sign that he was horny.

Phillip came around the corner. I lifted my hand and started to shift away from James.

His arm tightened around me. "Your son has given me his permission to make you happy."

More conflicting sensations danced in my chest and stomach. If only my emotions would get in line and present themselves one at a time.

"Not sure how I feel about being discussed behind my back." My words came out bitchier than I'd intended.

But they were both smiling. "It's a guy thing, Mom," Phillip said. He plopped down, cross-legged, on the hardwood floor in front of us.

I really need to get more furniture. If we're staying, that is.

A pang in my heart. This had become my home.

And if I don't end up in prison. That thought, which I'd been avoiding all evening, made my stomach clench.

"I've been thinking about what you asked." Phillip rubbed his hands on his jeans. "I know Dad always put education down, said you didn't need it if you were smart and knew what you were doing. But I think I'd kinda like to go to college." He raised his gaze to meet mine. "Would that be okay?"

I started to say of course it would, but James spoke before I could. "Three and a half million would buy one hell of a college education."

Some heat—the wrong kind—erupted in my chest again. Oh yeah, *that's* what I was mad about.

I moved slightly away from James. "I'd love for you to go to college, Phillip. But you still need to consider if you might want to go into Dad's business afterwards. It's hard to build up a business from the ground. You don't want to give up one that's already been constructed."

James chuckled. "No pun intended."

I faked a smile. "Do you know what you want to study?"

"No, not yet," my son said. "But pretty much everybody at school assumes they're going to college. Some know what they want to do after, but a lot of them figure they'll get a better idea of that when they've taken some courses."

"That's often how it works," James said. "I'd originally thought I'd be a lawyer, like my stepfather. I took an acting class on a whim, and here I am." He spread his arms wide.

I leaned forward and patted Phillip's knee. "You don't have to decide now about the company. But yes, I do want you to go to college. I think your father put down education because he was jealous of Mr. Torenson having a degree."

Phillip looked worried. "But he said the deal was only on the table for a little while. How would we pay for college without the money from the company?"

James leaned forward too, his shoulder brushing mine. "Son, you own half of that company. That's a given. If it's worth six million or more, I'm sure you will get some income from it. More than enough to pay tuition."

Relief washed over Phillip's face.

I stifled my irritation at James. "Besides," I said to my son, "your father's been talking about Mr. Torenson wanting to buy his half of the company for a long time. Dad wouldn't sell. So I doubt the offer to buy you out will go away. Mr. Torenson was bluffing. You take your time to think about what you want to do."

Phillip's face lit with a grin. "Thanks, Mom." He hopped up and left the room.

I waited until I heard the sounds of a computer game coming from the study. Then I pushed farther away from James and twisted around to face him.

It was time to get some things cleared up.

CHAPTER SEVENTEEN

Carrie

I should have taken a deep breath and thought through what I wanted to say. Maybe even waited until another time when I wasn't so tired.

Instead I blurted out, "I'd appreciate it if you didn't call Phillip *son*."

James's face fell. His eyes went wide. "Why?"

"Because he's not your son, but you seem to be taking on that role, without even asking me if that was okay."

James's lips pinched together. "I thought you'd be pleased that I was taking an interest in the boy."

"I am, to some extent, but you cross the line sometimes."

"I do? When?"

"Like when you tried to end the discussion with Torenson."

"The guy was giving me the creeps. I wanted him away from you. You've had enough to deal with lately. I wanted him out of our house." James froze, his eyes registering the poor choice of words.

"It's *my* house, James."

"Sorry." He shook his head slightly. "I know that, but I guess I'm feeling a bit protective of you right now." He reached out to touch my cheek.

I pulled back. "In case you haven't noticed, we're having an argument."

James's jaw tightened. "Are we? I thought it was a *discussion*. But I guess I was wrong."

"Look..." I put a hand on his arm.

He pulled back this time. I dropped the hand into my lap. He looked away, a muscle in his jaw throbbing.

Adrenaline surged. My body wanted to get up and run.

But I made myself stay still. *He is not Greg. I don't need to be afraid of him.*

My next thought scared me more than James's anger. *And if he is like Greg, now's the time to find out.*

Finally I took the deep breath I should've started with. "Look, I know you mean well. But you've stepped right into the man-of-the-house role, and I'm not sure I'm ready for that. I got married right out of high school, to a controlling, violent man. And for the last eight months, I've lived in fear that he would find me."

I paused, gathering my thoughts. James still had his head turned away, but his jaw was no longer as tense.

"I need some time, to find my balance." I realized the truth of the words as they came out of my mouth. "I need to figure out how to be me, before I can be part of a *we*."

James, still looking away, swallowed hard, his Adam's apple bobbing in his throat. "Is this the breaking-up speech." His tone was bitter.

My hand went out, clutching at his arm this time. "No! Of course not. I–"

He shrugged off my hand, jumped up and paced the room.

My stomach roiled at the sight of his face, twisted with pain and anger.

"I don't want things to change," I said carefully. "That's the point. I can't go forward just yet, but I'm not trying to go backward." I heard the desperation creeping into my voice.

What have I done? This wasn't what I'd intended at all. "I need you to slow down some, that's all."

He stopped, dropped his gaze to the floor, rubbed the back of his neck. He turned toward me. His eyes had the haunted look I'd seen too often during the weeks right after Annaleise's death.

On cue, wind chimes tinkled tentatively.

"Aw, shut up!" I snapped at the air, my eyes burning.

The wind chimes clunked faintly.

It freaked me out a little to have our lovers' quarrel witnessed by the ghost of his best friend. But James was ignoring her.

"I can't slow down." His words were choked. "I'm already there! I trusted you, so I let you in. All the way in."

I opened my mouth, but my throat had closed. Heat burned behind my eyes.

I tried again. "I love you, James. I'm just not ready to be part of a couple, not completely. Not yet."

He dropped his head, rubbed his neck again, then turned toward the door. "I gotta go. I need to think."

My vision blurred. I reached out a hand. "Wait, James!"

But he kept moving, shaking his head. "I'll see you tomorrow."

I wanted to rush after him, hold him, make him stay. My body felt like lead. I struggled up off the sofa but he was already at the door.

And then he was through it, before I was halfway across the room. I expected the door to slam, but it closed with a gentle click.

That's so like James.

I burst into tears in the middle of my empty living room.

———◆———

James

By the time I got to my own porch I'd gone from pain to anger and back to pain again. I stumbled through my front door and slammed it behind me.

She's overreacting. At first I assumed it was my own thought, but it was far too rational and insightful for my present state of mind.

Oh, James!

Now that was definitely a female voice, throaty with laughter.

"Now is not the time, Annaleise."

The wind chimes chattered merrily. *You're overreacting too.*

I ignored her critique of my reactions. "What do you mean about Carrie?"

No answer.

"She's overreacting to what?" I demanded.

The wind chimes, softer and more distant.

"I guess I get to figure that out for myself," I muttered as I went into the kitchen. I poured myself a glass of white wine and sat down at the table.

A small lamp at the end of the counter was on a timer. It was the only light in the room, its soft glow casting shadows in the corners. I took a sip, then swirled the wine in the glass. It caught some of the light and winked at me.

Oh James, you always were so fanciful. An older female voice, the tone indulgent rather than the strident derision of my childhood.

"Hi, Mom." I hadn't heard from her directly in weeks, only thought that I'd felt her presence. I'd wondered if she had moved on, gone into the light or whatever. What was keeping her tied to the earth?

I wasn't sure how to feel about her still being here. Sad for her, maybe a little relieved for my own sake. Who wouldn't want their mom around for all time, especially since death had mellowed her.

"I can't believe I'm sitting here talking to ghosts." I took another hearty swig of wine.

So what is Carrie overreacting to? She seems to think I'm trying to control her.

I shook my head, slouched down in my chair. I certainly had no desire to control her. I barely had a handle on my own life. But I certainly had jumped into the man-of-the-house role—she was right about that—taking responsibility for trying to keep everyone safe.

My chest tightened. At the time, decisions had to be made quickly. I ground my teeth. There was hardly time for a committee meeting. And she could've spoken up if she didn't like me taking charge.

Heat burned in my chest. She'd seemed happy enough to let me protect her when her jackass husband was gunning for both of us. And to get her a lawyer and cover her bail when she was accused of his murder.

The moon had gone behind a cloud. Total darkness reigned outside my kitchen window. The night was eerily still.

A sharp yip, in the distance. I sat up straighter. Had I imagined it?

I strained to hear.

Silence.

Had it been Ginger? Was she hurt?

I reached for the phone in my pocket, then stopped. She didn't want me taking charge, then fine, she could damn well call *me* if Ginger was lost or hurt.

I drained my wineglass and stomped off to bed.

Carrie

I'd read for a while, trying to settle my nerves and distract my mind from the fight with James. Finally I felt relaxed enough that I might be able to sleep.

I'd let Ginger out and gone upstairs to wash my face and brush my teeth.

I was in my nightgown, pulling an old robe from my closet, when it dawned on me that Ginger had been outside for a long time. Normally she came to the door and barked once when she was ready to come back in.

Struggling into the robe, I scooped up my phone from the night stand and hurried out the bedroom door. Downstairs, I nudged aside the curtains at the living room window, my heart in my throat.

Out of habit, I told myself. Greg was gone. I didn't need to be afraid of every shadow or mildly strange occurrence anymore.

The light from the floods on the front of the house showed most of the empty field encompassed by the dog's invisible fence, but there was a band of darkness beyond the light where she could be. Or had she gone around to the side of the house?

I cracked open the door and stuck my head out, called her name, whistled.

Nothing, not even rustling noises.

I closed and locked the front door, then went to the kitchen and flipped the light switch beside the back door. Peering out the window at my garden, I was flooded with the memory of Greg trying to choke me.

I shook off the anxiety and made myself open the door. Again I called and whistled.

Again, no response.

"What's up, Mom?"

I jumped a little.

Damn, I'm still a nervous wreck.

"Ginger isn't coming when I call. Guess I'll put my clothes back on and look for her."

Phillip's face paled. "You think that's a good idea? Dad's killer is still on the loose."

With all the stress of being arrested, arraigned, and now fighting with James, I had forgotten that reality. If neither Phillip nor I had killed Greg, then somebody else had. And the killer might not be finished with us.

My insides twisted with indecision. I called the dog's name again, as loud as I could.

No response.

If she was hurt out there somewhere, or caught on a branch again, I couldn't leave her overnight.

But Phillip was right. It really wasn't safe to go out in the dark looking for her.

My hand moved to my phone, stuffed into the torn pocket of the old robe—torn by Greg one night when I didn't answer his demands for sex fast enough.

The hand froze. *I can't call James.*

Hell, I'd just risked everything we had together to back him off, to make him stop trying to take charge in the name of protecting me. So now I'm going to run to him to go search for my dog?

Maybe not!

And it was no safer for him out there than it was for me. We didn't know the killer's agenda.

My chest so tight I couldn't catch my breath, I closed and locked the kitchen door.

I'm so sorry, Ginger.

James

My sleep had been restless, to say the least. I'd woken a couple of times early in the night, thinking I had heard Carrie's voice, one time calling Ginger's name. But I'd decided it had been a dream.

Then I woke at three and couldn't get back to sleep.

I had to go into DC early this morning for a costume fitting for the new play. Might as well hit the road now and get breakfast along the way.

I'd forgotten to return Carrie's gun to her last night—well, my gun technically, but I'd bought it for her. I could use that as an excuse later to stop by her house. Since I was going into DC, with stricter gun laws than Virginia, I unloaded the pistol, stashing it in the trunk and the bullets in my glove box. The last thing I wanted right now was another run in with the law.

The sky was turning from black to charcoal gray as I drove out of our shared lane. Something glinted in my headlights, on the ground beside where the lane met the main road. I made a mental note to check it out when I got home. Probably a soda can thrown out of a passing car.

I longed to call Carrie, but it was too early. So I turned on the Mustang's radio and found a classical music station. I vowed I wouldn't call her, just show up later to return the gun. She wanted space, I'd give her space.

The appointment was at seven, and I was out of there in forty-five minutes, having had every inch of my body carefully measured for the costume. Normally, I would stay in town for a while, look up Todd to see if he was free for lunch, but I was anxious to get back to Virginia. I didn't even stop at my apartment.

Once on the road, I couldn't hold out any longer. My throat a bit tight and my stomach twitching, I called Carrie.

No answer. It went to voicemail. I left a breezy, just-checking-in message.

The drive home seemed much longer today.

Despite my anxiety, I remembered the glinting light from this morning. I hate leaving debris by the road. It encourages other inconsiderate types to think our beautiful countryside was one big trash can.

I pulled the Mustang into the lane and stopped, put it in park. It only took a moment to find the metal that had reflected my headlights earlier.

It was a tag on a black dog's collar, the plastic box for the invisible fence attached. The collar was intact and unbuckled. It hadn't broken or slipped off.

Ginger's collar, removed by human hands.
A clanging sound in the distance.

CHAPTER EIGHTEEN

Carrie

I woke with a throbbing headache and a vague memory of a strange dream, filled with relentless fire bells and struggling with dark-clad aliens.

My body felt like lead. I managed to turn my head and look at my clock. Its screen was dark.

Wha'? My fuzzy brain finally figured out that we must have had a power failure during the night. I fumbled for my watch on the nightstand. Seven-forty.

I shot upright. Pain coursed through my skull. Clutching both sides of my head, I stared at the watch I'd dropped on the comforter. I'd gone to bed at a little after ten. No way I had slept almost ten hours.

Vague noises from somewhere in the house. Probably Ginger's claws on the hardwood floors.

Wait! She'd never come back last night. And it was way too early for Phillip to be up of his own free will. Had James let himself in and was making breakfast, to apologize for walking out last night?

I sniffed the air. No cooking odors. Instead a vague scent I couldn't place—kind of soapy and chemical.

Wind chimes clamored.

The fire bells! Annaleise had been trying to wake me up!

I sprang out of bed and grabbed my old robe. Ignoring my screaming brain cells, I raced for the stairs.

There was no doubt I was fully awake now, with the adrenaline that was coursing through my body. But my brain was still foggy.

The odor grew fainter as I ran down the steps. Near the kitchen, I caught a whiff of it again.

Sounds of movement from Phillip's room. I veered down the hall.

More noises, louder, from behind his door. Something heavy being dragged, a low grunt.

I raised a hand to knock.

No! An urgent whisper in my ear.

My hand froze. I whipped my head around but nothing was there.

My hand dropped to the knob. It wouldn't turn.

Fresh adrenaline jolted through my system.

A key scratched in the front door lock.

James

I'd grabbed the pistol from my trunk and quickly loaded it, before tearing down the lane and swinging the Mustang in behind Carrie's car in her driveway. Heart racing, I jumped out and ran for the porch.

Something was definitely off. The house had a closed-up feel, the curtains still drawn. With the fear gone that Greg was lurking in the woods, Carrie had made a point of opening them wide the last few mornings.

All was quiet, too quiet. Until the wind chimes clanged their warning.

I didn't ring the doorbell, just jammed my key into the lock.

Carrie stood at the entrance to the hallway in a tattered robe, eyes wide, a finger against her lips.

I moved quickly toward her, my mouth open to ask what was wrong.

She shook her head and backed up to Phillip's door, touched the knob and mouthed, "Locked."

Grunts and muted cursing from the other side of the door. A chair leg scraping.

I pulled the gun from my jacket pocket and motioned for Carrie to step back. Raising a foot in the air, I aimed for below the knob.

And almost fell on my butt when my shoe slamming against wood only made the door rattle. Breaking down doors isn't as easy as they make it look on TV. I jammed my back against the opposite wall of the hallway and tried again.

The door splintered but still didn't open.

"I'll take care of you next, bitch!" A snarling female voice from inside the room.

I reached through the ragged hole my foot had created and unlocked the door. Gun raised, I entered the room. "Freeze!" I yelled.

Phillip hung limply from the rafters, a noose around his neck, his feet resting on a wooden chair.

Toni Hamilton, all in black and breathing heavily, stood by the chair, muscles bulging in the arm that held the boy's sagging body up by the waistband of his sweats. Her other hand was grasping the back of the chair.

A string of curses came out of her mouth.

My breath caught in my throat. Praying the boy was alive, I closed the gap between me and the woman in one lunging stride.

Carrie

As James yanked the blonde away from the chair, I ran to my son. Circling his waist with my arms, I lifted his weight to take the pressure off his neck.

My cheek was jammed against his chest. A thumping noise—was it my own blood pounding in my ears or Phillip's heart beating?

I felt his chest expand and tears of relief stung my eyes. "Hang on, baby," I cried. "James, help me!"

"Be right there," he huffed out, breathing heavy.

I managed to turn my head far enough to see what he was doing. Twisting her arm behind her back, he'd forced the woman to sit on the floor. He quickly tied her arms to the leg of the desk with a twisted bed sheet.

Then he was beside me. "Hang onto him," he said unnecessarily.

I wasn't about to let my son go. Still pushing upward as hard as I could without squeezing him too tightly, I shifted to one side to give James room.

He placed his foot on the chair and stood up on it. His fingers struggled with the knot at Phillip's neck. It wouldn't give.

The wind chimes were clattering again. I shifted my feet, trying to brace myself better.

James slid both arms under Phillip's armpits. "I've got him. Hand me the gun. I threw it on the bed."

I found the pistol in the jumbled bedding and gave it to him, then resumed my position, holding Phillip's weight off of the thick rope noose.

The gun went off, the noise ear-shattering. Several small chunks of ceiling fell on the bed.

I looked up. James had shot the rope. He pocketed the gun and yanked at the remaining threads.

They broke. Phillip's upper body drooped over my shoulder. His feet slid off the chair. I staggered backward, determined not to drop my son.

Then James was next to me, helping me lower him to the bed. He clawed at the noose's knot, finally loosening it.

Phillip's eyes were closed, but his chest was moving rhythmically. Relief washed through me.

I spotted a white cloth on the floor and grabbed it up. It reeked of the strange soapy, chemical smell I'd caught a whiff of earlier.

The wind chimes clanked. I dropped the cloth as my head swam.

Look out! We both jerked around.

Bill Harris, in jeans and a dark flannel shirt, stood in the doorway, his gun in one hand. The other hand was wrapped around Toni's forearm.

"It's ketamine," he said, his tone casual. "One of the club drugs the kids are into now."

My mind did its detachment thing. *I didn't dream the black-clad alien.* It was Toni, and that's why I'd slept ten hours.

I glanced at the desk leg. The sheet hung in shreds. She apparently had a knife.

Of course she does. Greg had several hunting knives. No doubt, Toni had helped herself to at least two.

Anger slammed my brain back into my body. "How'd you get into my house?" I demanded of the woman.

At the same time, James said, "Thank God you're here, Bill!"

CHAPTER NINETEEN

James

Belatedly, it registered that the deputy's pistol was pointed at me.

"Sorry, James," Bill Harris said. "Drop your gun."

I went hollow inside, except for the fist that had closed around my heart. "What are you doing, Bill?"

Harris let go of the woman, then wrapped his arm around her shoulders and squeezed.

"This little lady and me..." He grinned. "We're partners."

Toni smiled up at him. "In more ways than one," she was almost purring, "we were married two days ago."

Harris waggled his pistol at me. "Come on. Don't make me shoot you. I can see the gun bulging in your pants pocket. Take it out slowly and throw it on the floor."

My chest filled with pressure and heat, felt like it was about to explode. Clenching my teeth, I carefully extracted the pistol from my pocket.

I had to think fast. I tossed the pistol behind me, heard it land with a thud somewhere on the far side of the bed.

Carrie stood by Phillip's feet, at the end of the bed. Given the opportunity, with a good lunge, she could probably get to the gun.

I planned to create that opportunity. "What–?"

Harris interrupted me. "To answer your question, Ms. Peterson. I disabled your alarm. So happens your main breaker's in a box on the side of your house. Not that unusual in older houses like this one." His tone was conversational.

It dawned on me that he was enjoying himself, showing off how clever he was. I felt nauseous. Why hadn't I seen this narcissistic streak in him before?

"Bolt cutters took care of the old padlock on it. Then I picked the locks on your back door, and Toni took it from there. She's quite light on her feet, snuck into both your rooms to administer the ketamine."

He squeezed the woman's shoulders again. She winced a little. "She must've miscalculated your dose though."

Toni opened her mouth. "She woke up–"

"Where's Ginger?" Carrie demanded, cutting off the woman's whining.

"Don't worry," Toni said. "She's safe. I'll take her home with me when we're done here." She sneered at Carrie. "You thought that was Greg texting you, didn't you? Sayin' he was gonna get ya. But it was me. We had it all planned out–"

Another shoulder squeeze from Harris. A bigger wince.

"We got things to take care of here, sweetie." Harris's voice sounded normal enough, but there was a hard edge under the surface.

Apparently he could gloat but she couldn't.

Toni looked up at him, her smile now a bit tentative.

"What are you going to do to us?" I said.

"Not sure about you two yet?" Harris waggled his gun again to include me and Carrie. "Ms. Peterson, move back."

She took two steps away from the end of the bed.

He nudged Toni toward me. "Now help her string the boy up again."

Yeah, right!

But I acted as if I was going to lift Phillip's torso from the bed. Toni reached for his feet.

When most of his weight was in the air, I gave his shoulders a mighty twist, rolling him off the bed on the other side. With Toni off balance, I was able to grab her and haul her in front of me, pinning her arms at her sides.

Harris laughed. "You've got to be kidding me." He lifted his pistol, moved his finger to the trigger.

I shoved the woman at him and dove to one side, jumping in front of Carrie.

"Bill," the woman shrieked as Harris's gun went off.

Toni Hamilton slid to the floor.

I knew my body made a lousy shield. We'd all be dead in seconds if I didn't come up with a plan, and a way to stall Harris until I could implement it.

Carrie

When Harris's gun roared, my heart stopped. I held my breath, waiting for James to crumple in front of me.

But he didn't. "Why'd you shoot her?" he yelled.

Meanwhile his right hand was extended behind him, waving at me, as he eased slightly back and to the left.

It dawned on my jangled brain that he was acting more shocked than he was, and he was trying to move us both closer to the gun behind the bed.

I prayed my son didn't wake up and try to play hero.

I leaned to the right, peeked around James's shoulder, hoping to draw Harris's eye in that direction, away from our target.

The Toni woman was lying on the floor, staring up at Harris, her mouth moving. No words came out. Blood soaked her black tee shirt, turning it even darker around the hole in her chest. She covered the wound with her hands but apparently had no strength to press down.

I felt a moment of pity for her, even though she'd tried to kill my son.

We nudged a fraction closer to our goal.

Harris was gazing down at her. Unfortunately, his gun was still pointed at us. "You really thought I would stay married to you, you stupid bitch." He lifted his head.

We froze.

He sneered. "She came into the sheriff's department a couple of weeks ago, describin' Peterson, askin' if we'd seen him around town. I took her into an interview room and was real sympathetic." He dragged out the last two words.

"She sobbed out the whole story, how the man she'd been livin' with said he was rich, owned a big company. He was gonna retire, take her to the Caribbean. He even changed his will, made her his heir after his son. Then the boy ran away, and the guy took off too, went after the kid."

Harris's gaze dropped to the woman again, but his gun hand didn't waver.

James eased us back and a little more to the left.

"When we called you out here," James said, "you intentionally didn't enforce the restraining order. You wanted Greg free, so you could kill him."

Harris looked at him, a self-satisfied smile on his face. "Yup. By then she was totally pissed at him, and I'd convinced her I was madly in love with her, and that we should kill him and take his money to the Caribbean ourselves. I'd found his campsite, and she went to him Sunday night, figurin' he would let her get close, wouldn't think she was a threat. I hung around in my cruiser up on the road, waitin' for one of you to find his corpse before I called for backup."

You bastard, I thought. *You let her do all the dirty work! While you hung back, so if anybody showed up, you could either run or pretend you were trying to intervene.* Just as he'd done here, letting her struggle with stringing Phillip up while he stayed outside.

I ducked my head behind James's broad back so my angry expression wouldn't distract Harris. We needed him to keep talking for a few more seconds. Looking down and to my left, I searched for the gun on the floor. There it was, halfway under the back corner of the bed.

"She even rigged that note on the boy's window," Harris was saying. "Meticulously traced the letters off a love letter Peterson had sent her once." He sounded almost proud of her, even though he'd just shot her. "See, we needed the boy to be accused of his father's murder so he couldn't inherit."

I peeked around James's right shoulder again.

Harris glared at me. "But you had to go and interfere," he said angrily, as if it was totally unreasonable for a mother to protect her child from a bogus murder rap. "You set it up so you got the blame... I thought I had him when I found his clothes you tried to hide."

I went cold inside.

"But the lab guy said it would be weeks. Gave me some bullshit about there already bein' an arrest, so processin' the evidence weren't a priority when he's got other open cases."

Harris chuckled. "Then I came up with this idea instead."

Apparently patience was not a virtue for this man.

Harris took a deep breath. "Okay, lemme think. I can still salvage this." He smiled. "I'll set it up to look like the boy and Toni shot it out." He paused, his face sobered. "But I still gotta figure out how to get rid of you two."

A moan of pain came from the woman.

Harris looked down at her. His gun hand dipped.

Now!

I tapped James's shoulder. He dove right, I went left.

I grabbed the pistol from the floor and rolled across the bed. The gun clasped in both hands, I sprang to my feet.

Harris was less than four feet away, his torso an easy target. And his gun was aimed at James.

A book levitated off the shelf and flew toward Harris. I squeezed the trigger just as the book hit his arm.

Two shots rang out.

My pistol bucked upward. I brought it back down, pointed at Harris, now lying on the floor, his gun a few feet from his hand.

James was crouched down behind the desk. My throat closed. Had he been hit?

He scuttled across the floor and grabbed the deputy's gun.

My knees wobbled with relief, but I was careful not to let my aim falter, even though the only sign of consciousness from Harris was a low groaning noise. Blood was pooling on the carpet beside him.

James stood and moved back several steps to stand beside me. "Damn, we make a good team!"

I snorted. "At least when it comes to shooting people." But my chest swelled with warmth.

He knew I was a better shot, and he'd set it up so I could get the gun. And Harris had reacted as most men would, assuming James was the threat, not me.

James turned his gaze to the man he'd thought was a friend. "Stupid fool. Never underestimate my woman."

Wind chimes tinkled.

One corner of James's mouth quirked up. "Excuse me. Never underestimate my *women*."

EPILOGUE

James

We sat on white wooden, folding chairs under a canvas canopy, beside a hole in the ground. Carrie on one side, Mary on the other, one auburn head, one blonde, both leaning into me some and clutching my hands. For Mary, I suspected this was dredging up memories of Annaleise and Charles's funeral not all that long ago.

It certainly was for me, although this was a much simpler affair, just a short graveside ceremony.

On a Monday afternoon, there weren't a lot of people in attendance. Even Sam hadn't been able to shake free from his commitments. I was fine with that. Mostly the funeral was for Phillip's benefit.

The rent-a-minister was droning on about a man he'd never met, and from the accolades he was throwing around, he hadn't bothered to find out anything about Gregory Peterson. He finally wound down with a prayer and we all muttered, "Amen."

He pulled a rose from the wreath Carrie had ordered in Phillip's name and walked over to the boy's chair, on the other side of his mother's. Handing the flower to Phillip, he gestured toward the grave.

The reverend pulled loose another rose and handed it to Carrie. She froze for a moment, then dropped my hand and took the flower. She stood and followed her son over to drop it into the hole, on top of Peterson's casket.

Mary and I rose to our feet. She squeezed my hand and let it go.

Carrie and her son came over to us, and I put an arm around each of their shoulders. We all stood silently for a moment, staring at the pile of dirt that two workmen were slowly shoveling into the grave.

Arms still around their shoulders, I started to turn us all toward my car, parked along the side of the cemetery road.

Carrie ducked out from under my arm with an apologetic smile. "Sorry, it's hard enough to walk on this grass in heels." She turned toward the road, leading the way.

I chuckled softly and squeezed Phillip's shoulders, then let him go. He gave me a weak smile and walked up next to his mother.

Mary, too thin in her plain navy dress, picked her way through the grass on Phillip's other side.

I slowed my pace, as Sheriff Wallace fell into step beside me.

Carrie glanced back over her shoulder but kept moving.

"I wanted to apologize for my deputy's actions," the sheriff drawled, when the others were a bit ahead of us.

"Not your fault, Sheriff."

"I know, but still..." He shook his head. "The man worked for me for ten years. I never would've thought he'd do somethin' like that."

"Three million's a small fortune," I said. "It would've let him retire in style."

Now it looked like he'd be retiring to the state penitentiary. Carrie's bullet had hit Harris in the left side of his chest. It had taken out a lung but hadn't been fatal.

He'd told the sheriff he'd found us trying to subdue Toni, who'd intended to hang the boy, staging it as a suicide. He'd been forced to shoot the woman, and we'd then misunderstood and thought he was attacking us.

He was right about one thing, the plan to stage Phillip's suicide. Toni had forged a suicide note, including a confession that he'd killed his father.

Definite premeditation on her part, but she hadn't lived to stand trial.

"I knew his story was hooey from the get-go," Sheriff Wallace said now. "Why would y'all think he was attacking you? You would've assumed he was there to save you."

An echo of the pressure in my chest three days ago, when I was staring at Bill Harris's gun. "That's exactly what I thought," I said to the sheriff.

He nodded. "But I had to go through the motions, you understand. Dot the i's and cross the t's, so he'll be convicted."

He had indeed put us through a bit of a wringer the last couple of days, with multiple interviews going over the events again and again.

"I understand, sir."

Thank God all the evidence had backed our story—the ketamine missing from the sheriff department's evidence room, Harris's prints on the bolt cutter still lying in the yard by the electric box beside Carrie's house. He'd probably figured he'd grab it when he turned the electricity back on after the suicide had been staged.

More damning evidence against Harris had been the trajectory of the bullets. The one in him had obviously come from where Carrie had said she was standing. While Harris's shot was aimed in my direction.

The sheriff assumed it went a little wild because Carrie got her shot off first.

We'd both refrained from mentioning the flying book.

We'd caught up with the others, standing next to my Mustang on the shoulder of the cemetery's winding lane.

The sheriff stuck out his hand to Carrie. "Sorry again for your loss, ma'am."

"Thank you." She shook his hand.

"So are y'all gonna be headin' back to Connecticut now?" He turned, offered his hand to Phillip.

The boy hesitated, then clasped the sheriff's hand firmly and shook it. "No, sir. We're staying here. Mom," he turned to Carrie, "I've decided I want to sell my half of the business. It'll pay for my college and then some."

"We need to get a new appraisal first," I said without thinking. "You can invest the proceeds and the rest will cover the start-up expenses of whatever kind of business you want later."

I looked at Carrie and swallowed hard. "That is, if that plan's okay with your mom."

She shook her head slightly, then smiled indulgently at me. "Sounds good."

The sheriff tipped his broad-brimmed hat at Carrie and Mary. "Y'all take care now." He shook my hand again and walked away.

Carrie slid her arm through mine. "I've always wanted to say this."

I smiled down at her. "What?"

"Home, James!"

Mary and Phillip groaned in unison.

Chuckling, I opened the back car door and gestured for them to climb in.

Once they had and I'd closed the door, I patted Carrie's hand on my arm. "Remember when you said you didn't trust your own judgement about who to trust?"

She nodded.

"Thanks to Harris, I totally get that now."

She gave me a sad smile and stood on tiptoe to kiss my cheek.

Carrie

James had put the top down and turned the radio way up so we could hear the music over the wind. It seemed wrong that we were so happy when we'd just buried someone, but we were. He kept touching my arm or grabbing my hand and squeezing it.

Even Phillip, sitting beside Mary in the backseat, seemed pleased. After all, he was riding in his dream car.

"All that food you brought," James yelled over his shoulder to Mary. "We should put it in my freezer. Maisie and the women from her church will no doubt be inundating us with offerings."

I glanced behind me. Mary was nodding, a smile lighting up her face. Her blue eyes sparkled.

It dawned on me that she was happy *for us*. My chest warmed.

James turned into our shared lane and pulled into my driveway. Something moved on the front porch.

I tensed, then recognized the flash of golden fur. "Ginger!" I shoved open the car door and took off across the lawn.

The dog had her nose down in a white casserole dish, scarfing up its contents. She was filthy. A piece of heavy twine was knotted around her neck. A length of it dangled, about five inches long, its end ragged.

Two other covered dishes were lined up next to the casserole. They looked undisturbed.

I grabbed the piece of twine and pulled her away from the dish. "No, girl," I said, but I couldn't help laughing. "That's people food." I didn't normally allow her table scraps since many seasonings aren't good for dogs.

I dropped to my knees and ran my hands over her body. "She doesn't seem to be hurt, but she's skin and bones."

"I've got a couple of steaks in the freezer," James said from behind me, a chuckle in his voice. "I think we should cook one up just for her tonight."

Phillip kneeled on the other side of the dog and rubbed her head. "Where were you, girl? We couldn't find you."

We'd searched all the woods and fields near our houses and had put up posters all around town, to no avail. I'd almost given up hope of ever seeing her again.

"Toni must've had her tied up somewhere," James said. "Maybe miles from here, but she found her way home."

Mary leaned in past Phillip's shoulder and pulled something lose from Ginger's hair. "This looks like insulation." She held the pink fuzz out on her fingertips.

James pointed toward the road. "There's an abandoned farm about five miles from here."

Beyond where we'd searched.

Mary shook her head. "I don't get it. That woman was willing to kill people..."

"Yeah," Phillip said, a sneer in his voice, "but she claimed to love animals. She told me once she'd worked for a vet when she was in high school."

Which is probably where she learned about ketamine. I'd looked it up on the Internet. One of its legitimate uses was as a veterinarian anesthesia.

I patted Ginger's head. "Let's get you a bath, and see about that steak."

"I'll get her, Mom. Come on, girl." Phillip took off for the backyard before I could remind him about his good clothes, which we'd just bought yesterday for his father's funeral.

Then I looked down at my own muddy black suit and shrugged.

James took my arm and helped me to my feet. Ignoring his own dress clothes, he wrapped his arms around me, mud and all. "Thank God she's safe," he said into my hair.

Movement out of the corner of my eye. Mary stepping off the porch. "I think I'll go get that steak out, and pop it in the microwave to thaw."

James tightened his arms around me. Warmth and a sense of peace slowly spread through my body.

"It's over," he said. "It's all over."

Wind chimes tinkled in a nonexistent breeze.

I smiled, my cheek crushed against his chest. I slid my arms around his waist and leaned into him. "Yes, it's over."

But it felt more like a beginning.

Excitement bubbled in my chest. Thirty-four years old and my life was finally getting started.

AUTHOR'S NOTES

If you enjoyed this story, please check out my other offerings at *misterio press* (https://misteriopress.com). Also, reviews are always appreciated! You can find links to leave one at your favorite book retailer(s) in the *misterio press* bookstore.

This is Book 2 in this trilogy. Book 1 is *Payback*, and Book 3 is *Backfire*.

We at *misterio press* take pride in putting out stories that are as free of errors as possible; therefore each of them is proofread multiple times by several people. But proofreaders are human. If you found any errors in this story, please email us at kass@kassandralamb.com so that they can be corrected. Thanks so much!

Much gratitude to my beta readers and my critique partners at *misterio press*, all of whom gave invaluable feedback that made this story better. Also a big thank you to my husband who is my final proofreader.

I hope you enjoyed reading this story as much as I enjoyed writing it. I loved going back into James and Carrie's world and bringing their Happy For Now ending from *Payback* to a Happily Ever After.

Well, they are almost there. They have a couple more bumps in the road to navigate in the next book, *Backfire*. But that story will focus on James's friend, Mary, who is trying to find love in the big city.

One of my goals with *Backlash* was to give readers an inside look at domestic violence. Those on the outside looking in sometimes can't understand why the woman doesn't "just leave."

But the situation is far more complicated than it might seem to be. First, batterers are often attracted to women who are insecure, whom they can easily manipulate. Then they sweep the woman off her feet, not giving her time to really get to know this new guy in her life.

Initially he hides his abusive tendencies, as best he can (although there are often small signs that the woman doesn't see, except in retrospect). Then once the hook is set and she's in love with him, perhaps even married to him, his true nature comes out.

He becomes more blatantly controlling and sets out to isolate her from family members or friends who might support her emotionally. He also tries to get her as dependent on him as possible, insisting she not work, maybe pushing her to get pregnant sooner instead of later, and only giving her enough money to barely cover the household expenses.

Abusers rarely set out to do all this with malice of forethought. They are often very insecure themselves. They've learned to cover and compensate for their insecurities by being charming at first to woo the woman, and then controlling her later to keep her from leaving.

I won't get into how men become abusers; that's another complicated story. But they usually aren't evil people, just really messed up.

Even though they put the woman down every chance they get, they're actually terrified deep inside that she will leave.

So in addition to controlling her, they make threats. These usually include that they will prove she's an unfit mother and take her kids away from her, that they'll cut her off without a cent, that no one else will ever love her because she's so worthless, etc. And the biggie, that they will track her down and kill her.

Sometimes that last threat is an empty one, but battered women have every reason to fear it's real. Every day, three or more women are killed in the U.S. by current or former male partners.

Some battered women certainly do get free from their abusive partners, more than those who are killed. As I said, batterers are usually not evil men, so they may not have the stomach to actually kill her, and/or they may be afraid of the legal consequences.

After a cooling-off period, they may get it that they're not getting her back, and/or they may very well move on themselves to a new partner/victim.

All too often, the woman who leaves ends up going back to the batterer. Again, those on the outside looking in think this is stupidity. Sometimes the woman is letting herself be fooled, because the man has turned on the charm again, telling her how sorry he is and how he'll never hurt her again. This is especially likely the first time she leaves and goes back.

But the number one reason given by women who go back is finances. When they haven't worked in years, have been told for all those years how worthless they are, and have no money of their own, they feel they have no choice, especially if they have kids to feed.

This is why hotlines and shelters are so, so important, to let women know they have other options.

And the efforts to prevent domestic violence and help survivors are working. Since 1994, when the Violence Against Women Act was enacted, the rate of serious intimate partner violence against women has gone down by 72%.

But we still have a long way to go.

National Domestic Violence Hotline • 1.800.799.SAFE (7233) • www.thehotline.org

~~

And here's a summary of Book 3, *Backfire*:

The road to hell is paved with good intentions.

Divorced from a verbally abusive man, Mary Hanson is long on loneliness and short on trust. When she finally goes out with a man she met through a dating service, a lovely evening culminates with a toe-curling kiss that fills her with hope.

Until the middle of the night when a rapist breaks into her apartment—a masked man who smells like her date's aftershave and knows things she has only told him.

Frantic, she turns to her friends, James and his girlfriend Carrie. To keep her safe, James brings Mary to his house in Virginia...without telling her that it's still occupied by the ghost of their mutual friend, who was murdered there months ago. But his good intentions backfire when the rapist follows Mary to the secluded property and attempts another attack.

With limited investigative skills, James must do his best to identify the stalker/rapist—is it the man Mary dated that night, or is it someone else pretending to be him? Because until James figures it out, Mary won't know who to trust...

And now Carrie and her teenage boy—whom James has begun to think of as a son—are at risk as well.

ABOUT THE AUTHOR

Jessica Dale is the alter ego of mystery writer, Kassandra Lamb.

Kassandra has always been passionate about two things, psychology and writing, and she also loves new challenges. After a successful career as a psychotherapist and college professor, she retired and started writing fiction, primarily mysteries.

Several years later, when she'd accumulated several plot ideas for romantic suspense stories, she decided it was time to branch out. And since some of those stories were a bit steamy, a new pen name seemed to be in order.

Thus, Jessica Dale was born. In addition to those steamier stories, she's completed the Unintended Consequences trilogy. These stories are sweet romance, but there is plenty of suspense and edge-of-your-seat excitement in them.

Readers can connect with Jessica via her alter ego at http s://kassandralamb.com. Also, you can sign up there for her newsletter to receive a heads-up when there are new releases, plus several free stories!

Kass/Jessica's email is kass@kassandralamb.com, and they both love hearing from readers!

Please check out these other great *misterio press* series:

Karma's A Bitch: Pet Psychic Mysteries
by Shannon Esposito
Multiple Motives: Kate Huntington Mysteries
by Kassandra Lamb
The Alchemical Detective: Riga Hayworth Paranormal
Mysteries
by Kirsten Weiss
Dangerous and Unseemly: Concordia Wells Historical
Mysteries
by K.B. Owen
Murder, Honey: Carol Sabala Mysteries
by Vinnie Hansen
Full Mortality: Nikki Latrelle Mysteries
by Sasscer Hill
Payback: Unintended Consequences Romantic Suspense
by Jessica Dale
Buried in the Dark: Frankie O'Farrell Mysteries
by Shannon Esposito
To Kill A Labrador: Marcia Banks and Buddy Cozy
Mysteries
by Kassandra Lamb
Lethal Assumptions: C.o.P. on the Scene Mysteries
by Kassandra Lamb
Never Sleep: Chronicles of a Lady Detective Historical
Mysteries
by K.B. Owen
Bound: Witches of Doyle Cozy Mysteries
by Kirsten Weiss

<u>At Wits' End: Doyle Cozy Mysteries</u>
by Kirsten Weiss
<u>Steeped In Murder: Tea and Tarot Mysteries</u>
by Kirsten Weiss
<u>Steam and Sensibility: Sensibility Grey Steampunk</u>
<u>Mysteries</u>
by Kirsten Weiss
<u>The Perfectly Proper Paranormal Museum Mysteries</u>
by Kirsten Weiss
<u>Big Shot: Big Murder Mysteries</u>
by Kirsten Weiss
Plus even more great mysteries/thrillers in the *misterio press* bookstore.

Milton Keynes UK
Ingram Content Group UK Ltd.
UKHW040706201123
432908UK00001B/131